UNDERCOVER GUARDIAN

BROTHERHOOD PROTECTORS WORLD

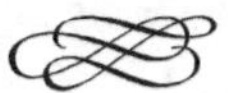

REGAN BLACK

Twisted Page Press LLC

Former Navy SEAL, Theo Tannehill, moved to the rural Black Hills of South Dakota for a fresh start. Becoming the sheriff wasn't part of the plan, but the job suits him and there's comfort in knowing the people in the community. When he discovers a totaled car packed with drugs and a dead body, he's determined to keep the criminal threat out of his town. That means vetting every new face, including a beautiful new mechanic.

Anna Lopez, a Guardian Agency protector who specializes in short-term urban assignments, is venturing away from her beloved Chicago to go undercover in the Black Hills. Posing as a mechanic, her role is to keep the sexy sheriff safe from the criminals wanting to take him out-- without letting him know she's covering his six.

Theo has questions and an increasing desire for the woman who always seems to be close when trouble strikes. But as the danger mounts, he must choose to trust Anna and her unique expertise or lose everything--including an unexpected chance at lasting love.

$$\sim$$

Visit ReganBlack.com for a full list of books, excerpts, and upcoming release dates.
For free reads, exclusive prizes, and much more, subscribe to Regan's monthly newsletter.

*As always, with special thanks to Elle James for inviting
me into her world of
Brotherhood Protectors.
And for those special people who go the extra mile to
make our world brighter.*

CHAPTER 1

MOODY NARCISSIST.

With a shake of her head, Anna Lopez tapped the backspace key and erased the inappropriate assessment of her latest client. Never smart to put derogatory opinions in writing.

She wasn't a psychiatrist, after all, just a bodyguard. Her bosses at the Guardian Agency were pros about discretion and privacy. Anna would have a chance to share her honest opinion during the in-person debrief. For the official paper trail, she needed to be more circumspect.

Client seemed preoccupied.

There, that was better. "Preoccupied with himself," she added under her breath.

The genius billionaire-of-the-day had been one of her less pleasant assignments. Arrogant and entitled, from her up-close vantage point he'd treated everyone in his path as a lesser being, barely worthy of his time and attention. Thank goodness he'd only requested local protection for his three days of meetings in Chicago. She would *not* want to be assigned to him fulltime.

Of course, Anna wasn't the protector they assigned long term. Her skills as a driver and her extensive knowledge of the Windy City made her invaluable, especially for transportation details.

That was one of her favorite aspects of this job. Not just loads of driving which she enjoyed in all its forms, but she never ran the risk of getting attached to the client. She never felt invested in one particular person beyond the moment. She wasn't built for that kind of connection anymore.

In the back pocket of her slacks, her phone vibrated. She hit save on the report and then checked the message.

Protect

The single-word text surprised her. Usually there was at least a day of downtime between assignments. Time to catch up on her laundry or— far more fun—grab lunch or a spa day with a friend. She finished her after-action report as swiftly as possible so she could go into the next job with a clear mind.

While she worked, she expected the string of messages that typically followed a protect order. Name and location and details about the client, but her phone remained eerily silent. After a speedy final read-through of her report, she submitted it.

Her phone hummed an instant later with a text message directing her to report to Patrick Gamble's office immediately.

She glanced around the empty office. Of course, the place was wired for security, but the timing felt like next-level supervision. With a mental head shake, she signed out of the program and shut down the computer. Picking up her purse and the coffee she hadn't quite finished, she headed for the elevator.

Gamble's office was one floor up in the posh building on Michigan Avenue. Gamble was one half of the law firm that managed the Guardian Agency. His partner, Nolan Swann, handled most of the protection assignments and Gamble spent more time recruiting personnel.

Of course, both men could hold their own in the field as well as they could in the court room. A fact some criminals had learned the hard way recently when Billie Hamilton, Gamble's ex-wife, had been targeted by a terrible enemy.

Anna had been part of the rescue and protection team and she'd loved every minute of the challenging case. She always got a thrill out of seeing justice served and this time around the crisis ended on a happier personal note as Billie and Patrick were planning to remarry soon.

Anna admired that kind of emotional courage.

With her purse over her shoulder and the cup of coffee in one hand, she was surprised to see Gamble's door wide open. She tapped her knuckles lightly on the glossy wood, waiting for his signal.

"Come in, Anna." His gaze was on his computer monitor. "Have a seat."

She did as he asked, setting her purse on the floor.

A moment later, Gamble turned, giving her his full attention and a wide smile. "Just skimmed your report. What did you really think of your last client?"

"Can't say I'm a fan," she replied. Gamble arched a dark eyebrow. "Fine. I found him to be a moody narcissist." She pressed her lips together to smother her amusement. "I rephrased for the official report."

He laughed. "Thanks for that. He's made some noise about something more like a full-time detail and I want to match him with the right team if that does happen." His amusement faded in the next moment. "Your next assignment, if you're interested, will likely be the polar opposite." He rested his folded hands on the desktop. "There are several factors in play and before I share details, I want to be sure you're up for it."

Since when was she not up for an assignment? "What kind of factors?"

"First, it's not in Chicago. It's a small-town placement and it's completely undercover. You'll be protecting a man who has resisted previous offers of help. His friends want to be sure someone is watching his back."

Her palms went damp. Small towns were nothing but social minefields and gossip mills in her experience. Not enough people and too much quiet. She ran her thumb over the cool hammered metal of the heirloom ring on her left index finger. "You're saying the man I'll be watching has no idea he's been overruled?"

"Correct. Ideally, you won't reveal your true purpose in the area."

Uh-huh. That could get dicey in a hurry. A new face in a small town would bring all kinds of attention. Not the greatest recipe for undercover success. "And?" She wanted the rest of the story, starting with why this guy was being overruled by his friends.

"Should you agree, I'll send all the details to your phone. If it helps, you'll be sent to the Black Hills of South Dakota, a few miles north of Sturgis. The timeline has room for you to drive yourself."

He knew how to push her buttons. She *loved* to drive and the travel would be the perfect break. Considered one of the best in the Guardian Agency, she actually trained new bodyguards on defensive driving. The Black Hills would be gorgeous this time of year with spring giving way to summer.

"What's the cover story? Or is that up to me?"

Gamble shook his head. "We have a couple of options, but I'm not getting into it until you're all-in. There's one dead body already and we've decided to work this solely on a need-to-know level."

"You think it will become a long-term thing." She took a slow breath. Her bosses had no reason to doubt her abilities on anything but staying power. Short and sweet was her wheelhouse.

"That's right. I'm sure it will go longer than a few days. I'm aware small towns aren't your preference."

She sat back in the chair and sipped her coffee. Did she really want this kind of a challenge? "So why even call me in?"

"Because the cover story plays better with a female protector."

An uncomfortable thought flitted through her mind. They wanted her to develop a relationship with the man who didn't want help. She'd rather walk a tightrope over a pool of hungry sharks. She forced a smile. "As long as you're not actually putting me out to pasture."

"No." He chuckled. "Not even close. Hank Patterson brought this to us. The person you'll be guarding is a friend of his, but he doesn't have any available women on his security team who can move into this role immediately."

"At least tell me the role."

Gamble gave a subtle nod. "You'll be fresh out of the Army on a cross country drive. You'll find a job and keep an eye on the client."

Find a job in a small town that was sure to distrust outsiders. Better and better. "The client who doesn't want protection."

"That's right." He gave her a hopeful look. "Think of it as an opportunity to get creative."

"And see the world." She sighed. "They gave me that same song and dance when I joined the Army," she joked. "Can I ask how Hank Patterson knows the client?"

"They worked special operations together."

Naturally. That did clear up a few things. Patterson had been a Navy SEAL and when he transitioned to civilian life again, he founded the Brotherhood Protectors, an elite personal security service. "You're telling me some former Spec Ops guy is hip-deep in trouble and Hank thinks a female bodyguard will be less noticeable."

"Pretty much. Hank is convinced his friend needs someone watching his back, whether he wants to admit it or not. He needs someone good who won't be recognized."

"All right." It definitely qualified as a challenge. She could manage a small town in the short term.

"I'll do it. As long as I get to come back to my comfy urban life as soon as the situation is stable."

"Absolutely."

She scooted her chair closer to the desk. "Tell me the rest of the story and I'll gear up and get on the road."

Gamble pulled a manila folder to the center of his desk and started walking her through the background and Patterson's reasons for concern.

She stifled an oath when she saw the population of just under fifteen-hundred people in Kite Creek. Didn't matter. She'd agreed. Besides, time and again she'd proven Anna Lopez didn't back down from any kind of fight.

CHAPTER 2

SHERIFF THEO TANNEHILL walked out of his office in the center of Kite Creek and crossed the street, headed toward the diner for a slice of pie and a cup of coffee. It was his preferred strategy to beat the afternoon slump. Most days in his jurisdiction were straightforward and calm, giving him ample time for this new habit.

He had zero complaints about that.

The bright welcome sign in the window and the cheery twinkle of sound from the bell over the door were more reminders that the recent trouble wasn't the norm around here. Kite Creek was quiet and peaceful and most folks didn't get into the kind of trouble that required his attention.

In fact, the current trouble he was trying to get under control came from outsiders. Everything pointed to a crew of drug runners that hadn't meant to get caught in his sleepy little county.

Soothing stability was what had drawn him to the area after a career of combat and training challenges with the SEAL teams. He'd tried to go home, but he hadn't felt like he fit into the hustle of Chicago any longer.

He'd traded in his sports car for a pickup truck and gone exploring instead. He met up with friends in a Deadwood, South Dakota casino and the area had grown on him. Joining the casino security team had been an effort to fill his time and when this sheriff's post opened up in the county to the north, he put his name on the ballot.

Surprisingly enough, the good folks of Kite Creek had voted him in.

Theo enjoyed the work, despite the worst part of the job—answering roadside emergencies. Drivers taking the curves too fast got themselves in all kinds of trouble. Those calls gave him some sleepless nights, dredged up ugly memories of tragedies during his days down range. Still wasn't enough to make him change his mind about his post.

Patty, the owner and namesake of the diner, was waiting for him when he reached the counter. Her steel-gray hair was held back from her face with a bright headband and her blue eyes sparkled behind the bright purple half-glasses perched at the end of her nose. "Time for the usual, Sheriff?" she asked as she set a white mug in front of him and filled it with fresh coffee.

"Yes, ma'am." He gave her a nod and a smile. "Any cherry pie left today?"

"One slice with your name on it. You want that á la mode?"

"Plain today." The pie habit was bad enough. If he didn't lay off the ice cream, he'd have to order jeans a size up. His buddies would never let him live that down.

Patty went into the kitchen to heat up his pie while Theo sipped his coffee. Another reason to come in here every day was to be as approachable as possible. He'd gotten the vote, but he wanted to keep their trust and that meant being available.

Considering the hornet's nest he'd managed to kick over a couple weeks ago, he wanted anyone with information or concerns to feel free to talk to him. He'd rolled up on what he thought was a single-car accident to find a popped trunk filled with cocaine and a body with two gunshot wounds and no identification.

Obviously, someone else had been driving the car when they'd lost control, but he had zero physical evidence for that person. The license plates had been stolen from a vehicle in Nebraska. The coroner had taken the body, but Theo had to take control of the drugs. Last he heard they still didn't have an ID on the body. The drugs, however, were locked up at the station since his first attempt to get them to the state lab had almost made him another statistic in the strange case.

The glaring lack of answers kept him on edge and irritable. He had yet to figure out how anyone had learned about the transfer. He trusted his two deputies, both of whom were lifelong residents of Kite Creek. None of the other locals were on his suspect list either. He kept searching and watching for any signs of trouble on his patrols, but kept coming up empty.

With tourist season heating up, more and more people were coming through his town and booking up the cabins that residents rented out. To make today even more fun, he'd just read an alert from state and federal agencies about a drug cartel moving product in and out of Canada.

It was enough to make him reconsider an offer of protection support from his old pal, Hank Patterson. As he dug into his slice of cherry pie, he debated opening that can of worms. The day he couldn't cover his own ass would be a grim day, indeed.

He turned as the bell jingled over the door. His pulse kicked at the sight of this particular new face. Anna Lopez had only been around for a little over a week, but it seemed she'd chosen to stay. Somehow, she'd talked her way into a job down at Shane's garage and day by day seemed to be winning over the hearts and minds of the locals.

"Hey, girl!" Patty called out, beaming as if she'd known Anna all her life. "Your order's about up."

Anna waved and smiled, but she was quickly diverted by Roger Cahill. The older man was a character with too much time on his hands now that he'd retired from long-haul trucking. He was on a mission to marry off his grandson, Alan, who also happened to be one of Theo's deputies.

Alan would be lucky to have Anna. She had patience with his grandfather, for starters. And she was pretty whether she wore her garage coveralls or street clothes. Her dark hair was usually pulled up in a high ponytail that swung when she walked. Her big brown eyes, framed by thick, long eyelashes, sparkled with enthusiasm whether the conversation was cars or the daily special. She carried herself with quiet confidence and those full lips often gave way to a fast and friendly smile.

He imagined she'd developed that confidence in the Army. Would've been necessary to hold her own in that environment. Shane had nothing but praise for her, claiming she went above and beyond to do a task right and knew her way around engines.

Theo had done a background search, as he did with anyone who stuck around more than a day or two. Hadn't found anything that put him on alert.

Her records matched the bits and pieces he heard her share. Like him, it seemed she'd opted to spend some time roaming the country after her military service.

Behind him, he heard Cahill quizzing her again. Couldn't fault the man's determination. "You still at the motel?" Cahill asked her.

"That's right," Anna replied.

"But, I showed you around and—"

Anna laughed and Theo glanced over in time to see her pat Cahill on the shoulder. "When I'm ready to sign a lease, you'll be the first to know."

Cahill had a small cottage at the edge of his property where his daughter had lived for a time. He must be hoping to put Anna close enough to bump into Alan more often. Theo smiled to himself over the man's not-so-subtle approach.

"Afternoon, sweetie," Patty said as Anna reached the counter. "I made up the sandwich of the day for you."

"Thanks so much. Can I get that to-go? And a chocolate milkshake for Shane, please."

Patty arched her brows. "Sure thing. Something wrong at the garage?"

"Not at all. I just dug into some long overdue reorganizing. If I stop for too long I won't want to finish." With an easy smile, she turned to Theo. "Having a good day, Sheriff?"

He swallowed his bite of the tart pie and raised

his coffee cup in a salute. Any day he didn't have to respond to a car wreck was a good day. "Pie makes every day perfect."

"So true."

Her voice was pleasant, but her dark eyes were somber. "Is Kite Creek too sedate for you?"

"Pardon?" Her eyebrows shot up and the clouds in her gaze disappeared. "Oh, no. Not at all. If I didn't like it, I'd move on."

Uh-huh. He forked up more pie. He wasn't in the mood to get attached to a semi-permanent resident. If she stuck, or started looking for a lease, he'd change his tune, try to get to know her a little better.

Finished with his pie and coffee, he tossed down cash to cover the bill just as Patty arrived with Anna's to-go order.

Somehow, they ended up walking to the door together and he opened it for her. They exited under the sweet jingle of the bell.

"Have a good afternoon," he said, pausing at the sidewalk.

"Shane tells me your vehicle is due for an oil change and tune up."

"Already?"

She nodded. "Needs to come in more often with the demands of mountain driving. According to Shane, 'country miles add up'. He asked me to remind you to drop it off."

He grinned, helpless against her spot-on impression of her new boss. "All right. I'll bring it in."

"Great. I'll let him know." She turned, walking down the block.

Theo had to jerk his attention up and away from the sexy sway of her denim-clad hips. The job and people kept him busy enough that he didn't feel lonely out here. Even when things were slow, there were people to talk to and various tasks to keep his mind sharp.

But Anna posed a temptation, got under his skin in a way he'd once welcomed. He wouldn't act on it. He wasn't ready to date, not seriously at any rate. It could be assumed that the minute he asked out any woman in town, rumors and speculation would start up. If he needed to blow off steam, he went to Deadwood to hang with his pals there.

He'd decided a while back this was going to be his place to sink new roots. Yes, he figured that meant a wife and kids. Eventually. He sure wasn't in a rush to get there. Good things came along for those who were patient.

Despite her new job, and familiar rapport with Patty and Grandpa Cahill, Anna gave off a temporary vibe. It was right there under the confidence and friendliness. He'd spotted the hint of wariness in her eyes and tension around her mouth when she didn't think anyone was looking. Maybe it came from working in a predominantly male industry, but he had a sense that she had one foot out the door, no matter how much she talked about liking Kite Creek.

Anna Lopez wasn't the right woman for him, no matter how much he enjoyed her pretty girl-next-door look with that subtle, underlying swagger. So why did he keep having this conversation with himself every damn time he ran into her?

Crossing the street, he focused on the short list of tasks he wanted to knock out this afternoon. Alan would be coming in to start the overnight shift in just a couple of hours and Theo had his personal truck if an emergency cropped up. This was as good a time as any to take the vehicle in for maintenance.

More than likely, Shane would have it back to him by morning.

Instead of walking into the station, Theo fished his keys from his pocket and drove the SUV three blocks down the hill to the garage. Anna was sitting on a stool eating her sandwich when he pulled up. All three of the service bays were empty. "Want me to come back later?"

Hopping to her feet, she set the sandwich aside. "Absolutely not." She seemed eager to get her hands on his car. "You can pull into the center bay."

He did as she asked and climbed out, handing her the key. "No rush on it. I've got my personal truck." Looking around, he could see she'd made some progress on the reorganization she mentioned to Patty.

"No rush?" She grinned. "You can see we aren't exactly overwhelmed with service appointments at the moment."

"Shane never seems to worry when things get slow." As if Theo was an expert on all business in town. He'd only been here eighteen months.

Anna cocked her head and laughed a little. "You're right. He seems content to get by as he is. Guess I'm used to staying busy."

The organizing proved as much. "I'll, um, leave you to it." Theo paused. "One condition."

Her dark brows lifted.

"Promise me you'll finish that sandwich first."

She winked. "Yes, sir."

Crap, now he felt like an old man and for some reason that made everything about this conversation with her more uncomfortable. "Right." He shook it off. "You know where to find me when you're done."

He walked back into the late afternoon sunshine and pulled out his sunglasses against the glare. Darkness fell fast and hard every day, but the last hour of sunlight was often a study in brutal angles before the sun set.

Traffic moved at its usual light pace along the

state highway that cut through the center of town. As Theo paused at a cross street, he heard the rev of an engine and turned toward the sound. Before he could register what was happening, he was tackled from the side and sliding through the strip of freshly-mown grass between the road and sidewalk.

The engine roared closer and then on screeching tires, the car slipped around the corner and zigzagged north, heading out of town.

"What the hell?" he asked when he got his breath back.

Anna was sprawled on top of him, a palm pressing into his shoulder, keeping him still, but her head was up, tracking the car that had nearly run him down. "I got the plate number." She murmured a series of letters and numbers under her breath.

"Louder." He prompted.

She rattled it off and he had it memorized too. "What state?"

"Nebraska."

Same as the stolen plate on the car he'd found. He hoped like hell this would turn out to be coincidence, but he wouldn't hold his breath. "Let me up and I'll go run a search." His hand was on the of swell of her hip and he yanked it away before he gave in and smoothed it over the sweet curve. "At the office," he added belatedly.

"What?" She looked down at him and then scrambled up and away as if he was on fire.

He might've been. Inappropriate or not, it had been impossible to ignore the softness of her body pinning him to the ground. The oil and grease from the shop couldn't mask the clean fragrance of her hair.

She was on her feet, extending a hand to help him. Did the woman always move so quickly?

He avoided her hand, getting to his feet on his own. He had more than a few years on her, but he wasn't Grandpa Cahill.

"Are you all right?" Her eyes were clear and sharp as she skimmed him head to toe and back up again.

His blood heated. Not the time for personal reactions. "What did you see?"

She turned away from him, stomping back toward the shop. He followed, determined to get her statement. "Anna!"

She scribbled something on a piece of paper and handed it to him. "Make, model and the plate number too."

"Thanks." She continued to scowl and he felt like a jerk for shouting at her. "Hey—"

"I didn't see anything as helpful as a face," she said with a gusty sigh. "Windows were tinted. Sorry."

"No worries about that. It happened so fast."

"She saved your life!" Shane came out of the front office. "Holy cow, Sheriff. That car was coming straight for you. If she hadn't been there…"

"Stop." Anna dodged her boss's praise. "It wasn't nearly that close."

Theo knew it had been exactly that close. He'd felt the heat of that engine a moment too late. Without her quick reactions, he might be waiting on an ambulance.

He cleared his throat. "You pick up anything with your security cameras, Shane?" One by one, he'd been encouraging the businesses to upgrade their security. If trouble was brewing, and his gut said it was, he wanted the best chance to gather good evidence.

"Oh, maybe so. Hadn't thought of it." He rushed into his office.

Theo studied Anna. The woman was already back at her workbench. She'd wrapped the remainder of her lunch and was zipping up her shapeless coveralls. "What are you doing?"

"Getting back to work." She barely spared him a glance.

"That's it? Just back to work?" After saving a life? His life. It didn't make sense. He expected more.

"Well, you're fine. Right?" She planted her hands on her hips, but her smile was tight and wobbled at one side.

Somehow that little sign of vulnerability reassured him. "Thanks to you, yes."

"Okay." She opened the driver's door and reached in to pop the hood of his official vehicle. "Good. You'll be wanting this back ASAP, right?"

Probably. "Take your time."

"I wasn't the one nearly flattened by a brand-new muscle car."

He checked the note she'd given him. Below the plate number, it was right there in her neat lettering: Dodge Charger, silver.

"Had the new taillight configuration," she was saying. "Just came out this year."

Huh. No wonder Shane had hired her so quickly. "Won't last long if the driver doesn't get some control."

"Agreed."

"Thank you doesn't seem like enough, Anna." He hooked his thumbs into his back pockets. "I really should've heard that engine in time."

"You did hear it. And turned toward it. You just didn't believe what you were seeing. Happens all the time in a crisis. The brain can't always process all the input, especially when it's something so wildly out of context."

"Where'd you pick up that information?"

She shrugged and moved around to the front of the car, stepping on the front bumper to get the hood brace in place so she could work. "Hard to tell. I like to learn new things."

"You're hiding something." Why not just tell him she'd learned it during her service days? Although he wasn't always into jawing about his experiences either.

She shook her head, her eyebrows drawing tight over that slim, straight nose. "Not intentionally." Turning from her study of his engine, she met his gaze. "It's trivia, Sheriff. Something I picked up when I worked with racing teams."

He hadn't seen anything like that in her background. "You worked with racing teams."

"One, primarily. A short-term gig. The overload of the senses, vision versus hearing in particular, came up during a driver's discussion about accidents on the track. Overwhelmed, the brain chooses what it thinks will be most useful to respond. A person will give details about what they saw and can't recall anything they heard. Or the reverse can be true."

It made sense. Unfortunately, he was feeling just vulnerable enough that her logic struck him like a bad sign. "Which team?"

"Pardon me?" She gave up her study of the engine and leaned against the front quarter panel. She looked as if she had nothing but time for him.

Unsettled, he dug in. "You said one primary racing team. Which one?"

"Army," she replied. "I spent a few weeks with the team on the truck circuit and I was lucky enough to sit in with the pit crew during one NASCAR race."

"That must've been something."

"It was the best. Let me know if I can do anything else. In the meantime, I'll be over here, under the hood." She aimed her thumb toward the engine waiting for her attention.

None of that racing experience had popped in his background search, probably because it was part of her service record. If she'd told Shane, the garage owner would've bragged about having a racing mechanic in the shop. A woman who knew cars and knew her way around engines might be involved in the recent trouble.

He turned toward Shane's office, determined not to let his quaking knees get the better of him, and had to stifle a groan. Every business owner between the garage and the sheriff's station was standing on the street watching him.

Watching out for him.

When he had the security footage from Shane's cameras in hand, he braced himself for the gauntlet of well-wishers.

CHAPTER 3

BETTER HIM THAN HER, Anna thought, eyeing the people who'd come out to check on the sheriff. It didn't surprise her in the least that the entire town wanted to verity that he was alive and well. One thing was clear from her first day in this quiet little community tucked into the Black Hills: they loved Sheriff Tannehill.

She definitely understood the appeal. He had the rugged good looks of a man who knew his way around life, good or bad. That hard, square jaw could be intimidating or friendly depending on the eyes and the smile. His nose had been broken a time or two and she wanted to know if it had happened in the field, during training, or during something more mundane like a bar fight.

Too easy to think of him throwing a haymaker with intent, though she struggled to picture Sheriff

Tannehill stepping one toe out of line. A bit easier to imagine it now. His eyes had been blazing when he'd gotten up after the near miss. The man had a temper. Somehow, seeing it flash made her like him even more.

"You okay?" Shane asked. "You can knock off early."

Because she'd done a good deed? If only he knew it was her real job. "I'm good." With a thumbs up and a grin, she hoped he'd let her be. She needed to get to her phone and send an update to Claudia. Hank had requested the top Guardian Agency tech support as well, having worked with her in the past.

Anna and Claudia had never met, but the woman was a wizard when it came to the research, oversight, and technical assistance she employed to support the protectors in the field. She'd helped Anna escape trouble plenty of times.

"You've got quick reflexes," Shane said, hovering as she worked. "We really could've lost Theo without you."

"The sheriff wouldn't want you spreading rumors like that." She shot him a wink. "It wasn't as close as it looked."

"Saw the tape. Closer than you think," Shane muttered. "But we don't want to bruise the man's pride."

"That's right."

"Need any help with this?"

"Don't think so." She patted the glossy black fender of the vehicle and decided to stroke her boss's ego too. "This might as well be brand new off the lot the way you've been taking care of it for him."

Shane grinned, pleased by the compliment. "We take care of our own. He's one of the good guys. Best sheriff we've had around here in years."

This was the first she'd heard of anything not being fabulous in the entirety of Kite Creek's existence. "You had trouble before?"

"Some trouble, yeah. Before Tannehill," he added in a hurry. "Out a ways there were reports of problems. Theft, gunshots and such. Started creeping closer to town. Sheriff Crowder couldn't seem to pin down a culprit. Then we discovered he'd been paid to look the other way."

"Wow. That's tough."

"Yup. State police turned over the entire department."

Which amounted to three deputies in addition to the new sheriff elected a year and a half ago. "Alan Cahill is that new?"

Shane bobbed his eyebrows. "Sounds as if you like that boy."

All she needed was her query about Alan getting back to Grandpa Cahill. That man was determined to see his grandson settled. He'd be waiting a long time if he expected Anna to fill the role of wife and mother. She enjoyed her freedom, and the bustle of a big city. And she wasn't romantically attracted to the fresh-faced Alan at all.

"Don't know him well enough to like him." She preferred *men* to boys, but that wasn't anything she wanted to discuss with her boss. "Deputy Cahill seems solid to me. I figured he'd been in the job a while."

"He's solid all right. But only on the job about a month longer than the sheriff. He happened to get through the academy and his training at just the right time for us."

Some of that should've been in the background intel, Anna thought. Probably would have been if they all weren't so dialed in on Tannehill himself.

"Well, I'd better get to it so the sheriff can have his official vehicle back."

"Holler if you need anything."

"I will." Grateful for the privacy, she finally sent a text about the incident to Claudia with all the details, adding what she'd just learned about the corrupt previous sheriff.

Halfway through changing the oil, her phone rang. Wiping her hands on a rag, she answered before it went to voice mail. "Hey, Claudia."

"Hey, yourself. I watched that video. Heck of an effort. Are you okay?"

Anna leaned back against the workbench. "It wasn't as close as it looked."

"Don't play humble with me," Claudia scolded. "I studied that video and found supporting angles."

Anna laughed. "Fine. It was close. But no one was hurt." Especially not the person she was here to protect.

"Thank goodness. The sheriff didn't look too happy."

"He would've been less happy if he'd been injured." The hospital was several miles away. If he'd been hit, it could have been fatal. "Tell me you have something."

"Possibly," Claudia allowed. "Thanks to the GPS tracker you put in place the other night, I think today's attempt to run him down might've been related to his last drive around the county. I'll keep digging into ownership and such, but there are two properties north and west of town that raise several questions for me."

Deeper into the mountains. Interesting. Cases were often small, patient steps that added up to solid information or evidence. "You're aware this isn't prime muscle car territory. Motorcycles, sure, with Sturgis being so close."

"The plates were fake and the owner of record on the registration might as well be another John Doe."

"Great. Seems brash for a drug runner or any

other kind of criminal to attack the sheriff with a car."

"He did seize a trunk-load of cocaine. I'd bet eight hours of uninterrupted sleep that whoever let that happen isn't willing to just write it off as a cost of doing business." Claudia chuckled and Anna knew she didn't resent the disruption of her new baby girl. "Kite Creek is a small town with a small force. They will try and recover their product. Stay close to him, Anna," Claudia said. "I don't have all the timing and connections lined up yet, but I suspect big trouble is on the way. An alert came down from the federal agencies about a noticeable increase in drug traffic moving through your area."

Great. She ended the call with that warning ringing in her head. A new alert would put the sheriff and his team on high alert, making a tricky job even more so.

She thought about the GPS report as she resumed work on the sheriff's vehicle. Maybe it was time to go for a drive herself. Except she wasn't out here as an investigator, she was here as a bodyguard. For a man who didn't believe he needed one.

Her hands busy with the tasks she knew inside and out, she mulled over various ways to get close to the sheriff. So far, she hadn't done much more than time her lunch breaks to his visits to Patty's diner. The man took an active interest in the people he'd sworn to protect. Naturally, balanced on a solid foundation of truth, her background had held up to the search he'd definitely conducted to verify her name and purpose in his town.

The Guardian Agency didn't do anything in half measures.

The Army service story had clearly appealed to Tannehill, who had also gone searching after his military career ended. Talking her way into this job at the garage had been the biggest challenge, but it gave her an excellent view of the main drag. And she liked working on cars of any size and shape. Given a choice, she'd still be on duty in the motor pool for Uncle Sam.

As the afternoon edged toward evening and the sun leaned into the horizon, she started thinking ahead to driving out to Tannehill's house in the dark. Granted, she'd only been here a little over a week, but she still wasn't used to how the sunlight went out like someone flipped a switch in the mountains.

It was a little eerie to go from beautiful colors sweeping the sky to star-studded velvet. That and the quiet. Who knew all that comfort she felt in Chicago came from the ambient noise of people and traffic? In the solitude of keeping watch over the sheriff, she could almost hear the trees growing. It wasn't awful, just different.

"Hey, Anna. You got company."

She rolled out from under the sheriff's vehicle

to see a small crowd of people gathered in front of the service bays. Patty seemed to be in the lead, holding a white take out bag and one of the tall foam cups she used for milkshakes. Beside her, Grandpa Cahill held a clamshell box.

"What's all this?" Never eager to be in the limelight, she twisted a work rag in her hands, willing her nerves to settle.

"It's a thank you," Patty began, her voice cracking. "You saved Sheriff Tannehill today."

"Oh, I—" This was not conducive to the low profile she'd been trying to maintain. "Any one of you would've done the same."

"But we didn't." Patty stepped forward. "*You* did. We brought you the dinner special, a lemon freeze, and strawberry shortcake for dessert."

Those lemon freeze treats had become a weakness. "Patty, you didn't need to do this."

"She did," Grandpa Cahill interjected. "Shows all her feelings with food. This is a small token of how much we all appreciate what you did."

"Guys, really." No amount of protesting was going to end this quickly. Resigned, she smiled and tried to relax in the moment. "You're all too good to me. Thanks."

She accepted the bag, box, and lemon freeze, along with plenty of pats on the back before the crowd drifted away.

"You should go on home for the night," Shane

said as his security lights winked on. "I can finish up."

"I've got it," she insisted.

"You've already had one meal in the shop today. Two is probably a violation or something."

She smothered a laugh, recognizing an unwinnable argument. "Fine. But let's both go home. I'll finish this in the morning and take it over. Sheriff Tannehill said he wasn't in a big hurry."

Shane seemed to debate this information. "All right, it's a deal. Lisa's been wanting me home earlier."

Anna grinned. "Then go make her happy." She cleaned up her workspace while Shane pulled the bay doors down and locked them. Within minutes they were both headed out. Him to his wife and her to the motel room. After dinner and a change of clothes, she'd have dessert in the car before hiking up to the spot that gave her a good overview of Tannehill's house.

CHAPTER 4

"Looks like this one's for you, Sheriff," Deputy Cahill called out.

"What makes you say that?" Theo fought off a wave of annoyance and turned from his computer.

He'd been searching for a trace of the car that had nearly flattened him yesterday afternoon. The license plate, as expected, was bogus, reported stolen from a vehicle at a rest stop in Nebraska. Surely a car built for speed had been caught by another department in the area, but so far, he had nothing to go on.

In the office doorway, Cahill wore a lopsided grin. "Well, it's your SUV that just arrived and that cute new mechanic is behind the wheel."

Cute wasn't how he'd describe Anna Lopez at all. She sure hadn't tackled him with cute power. He doubted she'd appreciate the description either, but he'd let them sort it out as they got acquainted. It was a foregone conclusion that Cahill would ask her out, if only to appease his grandfather.

Romance wasn't Theo's specialty but he didn't think the two of them would suit. "You can take the keys for me," he suggested. Just in case Grandpa Cahill was watching from Patty's window.

"No, thanks." Cahill held up his hands. "If I go out there Grandpa will read way too much into it." He fiddled with his radio, pretending to listen. "Did you hear that? West needs backup."

Theo hadn't heard anything but static and he laughed as Cahill took off like his shoes were on fire.

The sheriff's station was compact, to put a polite spin on it. He stepped into the lobby from the short hallway just as Anna walked in. She pushed her sunglasses to the top of her head and looked around, her eyes landing on him. His skin went warm.

"Hi," she said. "Your vehicle is all set."

No, he didn't find her cute at all. Gorgeous was more like it. As usual, her thick hair was pulled back and her dark brown eyes sparkled with that clear friendliness that seemed to draw people in. Tempting, that's what she was. She wore a bright blue tank top that showed off her toned arms and a healthy amount of cleavage, tucked into jeans that were faded in the right places, and work boots, probably steel-toed for safety. Since when did he find such a workaday look so sexy?

Since Anna, apparently.

A few years ago, he would've made a move. Now that kind of thing had to wait. The safety of an entire community was riding on his decisions. Bottom line, she was still a stranger even though she'd been accepted by everyone from the moment she'd rolled into town.

She hadn't been evasive in any conversation he'd had with her, but Theo believed in giving people enough time to show their true colors. It was a lesson learned the hard way during his military career.

"Sheriff?" She cocked her head. "Is there a problem?"

"No." He forced his lips into what he hoped was a friendly smile. "Just caught me thinking. You didn't have to deliver it."

"I wanted a change of scenery."

She smiled and he felt it as vividly as a caress. Yeah, the new mechanic was temptation all right. His pulse kicked and he discovered he was glad Cahill had run off.

"Three blocks makes that much of a difference?"

"Around here, you know it does." Stepping forward, she handed him the keys over the counter. "Every bend in the road seems to show off something new and spectacular. I didn't expect to enjoy the area so much when I arrived."

He was close enough now to catch a whiff of her shampoo tangled up with the smells of the garage. It was surprisingly pleasant. "From Chicago, right?"

"That's right." Another smile. Another kick of his pulse. "Well, you're all set. We checked out all the systems and did the works from tire rotation all the way up to new windshield wiper blades. Let me know if you have any trouble, Sheriff."

He didn't want her to go. "Call me Theo." The friendly smile on her face wobbled ever so slightly. "Everyone does," he added. Everyone who wasn't a criminal anyway. "Where did you learn to work on cars?"

"According to my mother, it's in my DNA by way of my dad and hers. Double whammy." She chuckled and her gaze softened. He'd have to check to see if her parents were still living. "Then the Army rounded out my training, taught me everything my family hadn't."

"Your mechanically-inclined relatives didn't know everything?"

She laughed again and he thought he could get addicted to that sound, to the enthusiasm in her eyes that made her laughter all the sweeter. He gave himself a mental shake. What was wrong with him?

"Actually, they did, but the people in charge of

the training like to feel important." She winked. "It wasn't like I'd serviced MRAPs on a weekly basis before the military."

Theo leaned his forearms on the counter, putting him eye level with her. "Sounds like you enjoyed your career."

"I did." She bobbed her head and took a step back. "I should get back before Shane feels obligated to start on the oil change. He set aside today to search for parts for his new project."

"He must be thrilled to have you on board so he can focus on the fun stuff."

"Guess so. It sure works for me." She turned, giving him a tantalizing view of her sexy backside. Pausing at the door, she said, "Be safe out there."

"You, too." He called after her, but the door was already swinging shut.

It opened again. "Forgot to warn you." She grinned sheepishly. "You'll need to adjust your seat and mirrors. I couldn't make it even three blocks on your settings. I put the seat all the way back so you can get in it, but it's not where you like it." With another quick laugh and a wave, she was gone.

Well, if Cahill wasn't interested in asking her out, Theo might have to do so. Assuming he didn't find any red flags during a deeper dive into her background.

FOR THE REST of the day, Anna busied herself with organizing and cleaning up the garage until it was time to jog up to Patty's for an afternoon snack and her requisite run-in with the sheriff. In her mind, it was an official check-in, though she made it as coincidental as possible each day. Paired with Claudia's not-entirely-legal tap into the security system at the sheriff's station, Anna felt as if she had a pretty good handle on his movements around town.

She also had an app on her phone that alerted her to any emergency calls and the first responders dispatched to an incident. Until she came up with a better reason to stay on the sheriff's hip, it was the best she could do while maintaining her cover. Other than yesterday's drama, nothing much had been happening in the immediate area.

Usually, that would put her more on edge, but frankly she was grateful for the time it gave her to get settled and accustomed to the area. Basic research had quickly eliminated most of Kite Creek's residents as threats to Tannehill. By chatting up Grandpa Cahill on her frequent visits to Patty's, she'd gained loads of intel. The man was a font of information on the current and prior folks in the county.

Didn't hurt her cause that he'd decided she

should marry his remaining available grandson. He seemed to be operating on the theory that if he gave her all the Kite Creek history, she'd want to be part of its future.

She could hardly brush him off or deny her interest in his grandson without cutting off her best source of local intel. Time and again, he'd shared tales of the sheriff's run-ins with rowdy tourists and the one or two black sheep of the small town.

It was a fresh new sensation for Anna to not be a name on that list. She was pretty sure the small town where she'd been raised still considered her name synonymous with trouble. Being the girl who worked on cars alongside her dad and brothers, the girl who preferred engines to dance class, made her different, and that was all the ammunition anyone needed to stir up rumors and speculation.

Gossip had ranged from her sexual identity—as if it was anyone's business—to her intelligence or lack thereof. Developing a figure in her early teens hadn't helped anything. Though it hurt to leave her family, she'd been so eager to move on and so willing to believe things would change once she did.

Wrong again, Lopez.

She'd proven herself more than capable as a soldier and a mechanic from day one in the Army. If only being good at her job could also eliminate jerks and bullies from the world. Thankfully, the Guardian Agency had picked her up and given her a new way to make an impact after her career came to a screeching halt over an unprovable complaint of sexual harassment.

There was gossip in Kite Creek about her as a newcomer, but so far, she hadn't made any big blunders that drew the wrong kind of attention. Here, people seemed to like her as she was. Refreshing. Although it was a bit of a weird full circle kind of moment, she was grateful she didn't need to fight any other rumors while trying to keep the sheriff safe.

She'd just called in the order for herself and Shane when he walked into the service area. "Just got a call from a wrecker bringing us a Camaro sporting a flat tire," Shane said. "Let me know if you need a hand."

"I'll manage." She smiled and shrugged her coveralls back up over her shoulders. "Our order should be ready at Patty's in about ten minutes."

Shane bobbed his head. "I'll grab that."

Anna's intuition was prickling before the wrecker pulled into view. A muscle car with a flat tire seemed like a big coincidence after another muscle car nearly took out the sheriff yesterday. Sure, plenty of thrill seekers pushed their skills too far on the roads out here, but still.

She made a note of the license plate and carefully evaluated the Camaro driver as he hopped down from the cab of the tow truck.

"You're the mechanic?" The man gave her a lengthy elevator look up and down her body.

She ignored it. "That's right." She walked around his car. "I don't have the same brand of tires you're riding on right now, but I can order them for you. It would take forty-eight hours."

He shook his head, his gaze lingering, as if he was sure he could see right through her coveralls.

The fighter in her was ready. Jerks like this were a dime a dozen. Her dislike for him went beyond his sexist attitude about who might be capable of fixing a car. He was just a shade too slick for this area. Too watchful and his mouth seemed locked in a perpetual sneer.

"Nah," he said at last. "Just give me two of the right size. I need to get back on the road."

"Vacation?" she asked as she wrote it up.

"Nah, not really." This time, his gaze raked over the town, his mouth still fixed in that disparaging sneer. "The guys and I head to Deadwood pretty regular."

She could see this guy slouched at a poker table, all attitude and bluff. But something else put her on edge. It was like he was casing the area. "We'll get you going again." She gave him a price and had to hide her disappointment when he paid in cash. A credit card might've led to a lead.

Did he know that or was she just suspicious of everyone?

She had his name, assuming it was real. And she had his car. Directing him to the outside waiting area, she suggested he head up to Patty's for refreshment while she did the work.

What she wouldn't give for a K9 officer trained for drugs to stroll by about now. In Chicago, she could've made a call. Out here, she was on her own.

Gamble believed in her, so she'd keep on believing in herself.

Rather than give her a reprieve, the driver stayed near the garage, sunglasses over his eyes, making a couple of phone calls while he waited. Worse, his proximity made it difficult for her to conduct a thorough search of his car. When she had the tires on, she backed the car out of the bay and returned his keys.

"Drive safe and good luck at the casinos," she said.

He lifted his chin and gave her another one of those long looks that creeped her out despite her confidence in her hand-to-hand combat skills.

When he finally pulled away, heading south toward Deadwood, she breathed easier.

Her stomach was too jumpy for food, so she carried what should've been lunch back to her motel room when they closed the garage. Once she'd cleaned up, she downed a soda and half of the meatball sub that had been the sandwich of the day. The quick hit of caffeine and sugar along with the spicy meatballs put her back in the right frame of mind. Just in case it was connected, she sent Claudia the few details she had on the Camaro and the driver while she waited for it to get dark enough to drive out to keep an eye on the sheriff.

The immediate ringing of her phone startled her. "Hey, Claudia," she answered.

"Hey yourself. I've been doing some reverse engineering since that alert came down from the feds. There is definitely a drug relay running close by and likely coming through at regular intervals. As soon as I have more info I'll send it along. That Camaro you serviced fits the profile of the crew I'm pulling together."

Anna knew that driver had been trouble. Frustrated, she paced the room. "I couldn't search the car, he was hanging too close."

"No worries. I know your focus is Tannehill's safety, but it's always good to know the enemy."

"Definitely true."

The man was stubborn, Anna thought an hour later from her vantage point in the trees behind his house a few hours later. Good thing she didn't mind roughing it for the sake of a case. She didn't understand him. He refused the offer of direct protection and yet, despite the threat, he didn't have a security system in place at his home. It wasn't as if he lived off the grid, anyone could find him with a few questions or some legwork. The two floodlights, one at the driveway and one at the corner that covered the back door, didn't count as security.

Her interpretation of the case file didn't imply that this drug crew would be bothered by the sudden glare of a light.

Especially since the sheriff's home was all but isolated out here. One road in and out. At least she didn't have to worry about staying in shape. Hiking to her hiding place each night was plenty of cardio with a booster shot of incline.

Once again, the sheriff—Theo—was home. She guessed he was kicked back watching television based on the glow of the lights against the closed curtains. Around eleven, as it happened most nights, the glow of the TV went out. Lights flicked off in the rest of the house and a softer light came on in his bedroom.

A few minutes later everything was dark and Anna had to fight back her curiosity about the man behind the badge. Not her business if he slept in boxers or nothing at all. She had no reason to speculate if the room was big enough for a king bed so he could stretch out, or if he had to make due with a queen.

No way anything smaller would be comfortable for a man of his size.

Good grief, she had a bad case of infatuation with Theo. That just felt like such a personal step. Like they were friends, but they weren't. She couldn't even be honest with him about why she'd come to town.

Irritated with herself, she focused on more important questions, like why he'd settled in this tiny little town or how he expected to fight off a crew that wanted him out of the way so they could reclaim the drugs he'd seized.

The low rumble of an engine on the highway was followed by more silence. Sound traveled differently out here in the mountains than it did in the city. The lack of ambient noise had been uncomfortable at first, especially during her night watch, but she was slowly starting to appreciate it.

The dropping temperature had her blowing into her hands to ease the chill. She hadn't packed gloves and needed to rectify that error soon. Up here the nights didn't seem to realize it was almost summer.

When she heard the snap of a twig, she held her breath and braced for trouble. The sound was in front of her, between her and the house. Sure enough, a shadow moved, a two-legged predator sneaking around the back yard.

That was not gonna fly, not on her watch.

One on one, she could take pretty much any kind of assailant. If this person thought the sheriff would be alone, easily overcome and subdued, they were in for a shock. Theo gave off an easygoing, laid back vibe, but the man was a former SEAL and rusty or not, he had some skills under the approachable façade. Still, she wouldn't hesitate to intervene, not only due to her orders, but because an ambush offended her sense of fair play.

Unfortunately, this could get tricky. She knew her limits. Ask her to track anyone through the city and she could do it without getting caught, but out here, she wouldn't be any stealthier than the person currently searching for a way inside Theo's home.

Somehow, she had to prevent disaster. Preferably without getting caught herself.

To her aggravation, the person stalking Theo's house managed to avoid tripping the lights on their way to a lower-level window. Hiding the glow of her phone, she did a search for wolf calls and turned her volume up, hoping the sound would carry to the perp.

The person stopped moving for only a moment. It was enough time for Anna to find a rock. She popped to her feet and hurled it at the house, hoping to get close enough to spook the prowler. Quickly shuffling away from her hiding spot, she moved closer and threw another stone, this time hitting the back door.

No lights came on, but the prowler was scanning the woods, momentarily distracted. She played the wolf call again.

This time the prowler pulled out his phone. She was too far away to see any facial features from the glow of the screen. After several terse seconds he pocketed the device and resumed his attempt to break in.

She heard the soft squeak as the glass popped out of the window frame. Anna sent an emergency text to Claudia, begging her to call the sheriff's phone and wake him up.

Praying she wouldn't blow her entire mission, she raced toward the house, tripping the motion-activated flood light and launching herself at the prowler. They tumbled, rolled and she caught his foot, wrenching his ankle. Then she was up and running away, the prowler's pained cry echoing behind her.

CHAPTER 5

THEO WOKE IMMEDIATELY when his cell phone rang. He sat up and checked the screen, but the number was listed as "unknown". He swiped to answer the call. "Hello?" The line was open, but no one spoke. "Hello? You've reached Sheriff Tannehill."

Noticing the floodlights were on in his back yard, he rolled out of bed. Grabbing his jeans, he yanked them up as he kept asking the caller to speak. When something outside screamed, Theo ended the bogus call, took his gun out of the lock box and rushed to the back door.

Usually, when that light went on it was thanks to a deer wandering by or a raccoon getting too hopeful about an easy snack. As long as he'd lived here, he'd never heard an animal cry out like that.

He called the station and Cahill, on duty overnight, picked up.

"Get to my place," Theo ordered. "Possible break-in in progress." He ended the call before Cahill could confirm any more details.

Silencing his phone, he shoved it into his pocket and went to protect his home. Opening the back door, slowly, he stepped outside to listen. Hearing muffled sounds around the corner, he padded down the steps for a closer look.

"Who's there?" he shouted into the night.

Whoever—or whatever—had tripped the security light was now out of sight in the trees. Cautiously, Theo gave chase to the edge of his security lighting. He wasn't an idiot and couldn't afford to go out there barefoot, with only his handgun. The immediate threat to the house seemed to be gone, but as he walked around, using his phone as a flashlight, he found two sets of prints as well as a broken basement window.

He supposed this was his last night winning the argument against a security system. He'd have to get someone out here right away or listen to everyone in town nag him once word of tonight's attack got out.

After taking a couple of pictures of the footprints and the broken window, he went inside to finish dressing before Cahill arrived.

～

If Anna hadn't done her full recon duty each night upon arrival, she never would've escaped undetected. Thankfully, she had and knew just where to turn, even on a dark night, to get back to her vehicle without being seen. It seemed the prowler had been more interested in getting away than following her.

She hoped every step was agony for that jerk. He deserved worse for going after the sheriff at home. If the stars lined up, maybe Theo had caught the prowler by now and he and his team could put an end to the criminals harassing him.

She was convinced the attempt to run him over and now this attempted home invasion were connected and related to the drugs Theo had seized. No one else had motive to go after him.

Reaching her truck, she waited long enough to be sure she hadn't been followed. A quick walka-round of the vehicle confirmed no one had tampered with it. She couldn't go back to the motel until she knew Theo was okay. So, foolish or not, she risked her cover and turned down the road toward the sheriff's house.

Deputy Cahill was there, lights flashing on his vehicle casting a red and blue glow over the house. She pulled onto the shoulder and parked, then hopped out and walked up the driveway. "Everything okay here?"

Both men turned at the same time, wearing similar expressions of confusion. "Anna?" Cahill was in uniform, Theo wore a T-shirt with the logo of a popular band, along with jeans and tennis shoes that weren't tied. His jaw was shadowed with stubble and his gaze was as sharp as a knife. It shouldn't be an enticing look, but she couldn't drag her eyes away from him.

"What are you doing out here?" Theo asked, recovering first.

"Taking a late drive. Helps me unwind so I can sleep." Mostly truth.

Did the sheriff blanch? Had to be an effect of the emergency lighting. "You need to be careful on the roads."

"Always," she assured him. "I saw the lights and thought maybe I could help."

"Still in service mode?" Theo hooked his thumbs in front pockets.

"I guess so." She smiled, watched his shoulders relax. Given a chance, she wouldn't mind digging her fingers into those firm muscles. "Did someone get hurt?"

"No, no injuries." Theo grimaced. "We're waiting on a tracking team. Unless you know how to do that too."

"Not my forte," she admitted. "What happened?"

"Someone was snooping around," he replied,

shoving at his hair. "Broke a window and, yes, they got away. Barely." He planted his hands on his lean hips. "We'll find him."

"Of course you will." She aimed her most confident smile his way. "If you're good here, I guess I'll leave you to it."

She felt a hundred times better seeing him in one piece. Heading down the driveway to her truck, she was surprised to hear him following her.

"Something else, Sheriff?"

"You need to be careful," he said. "These roads can be dangerous. Especially at night."

Especially with a crew of drug mules making regular runs through the area. "I'll be safe."

She wished she could tell him the truth about her driving skills and…everything else. It burned her pride to keep secrets about her real purpose, even though she knew he'd resist her help if she confessed.

"Anna?" His eyebrows flexed into a frown only made more fierce by the shadows. "Why are you really out here?"

"Late night drive, as I said. I saw the lights." She opened her door, but didn't climb into the driver's seat just yet. "Didn't realize this was your place."

He braced his hands on the door and the truck, caging her in. "I didn't say it was," he said, wary now.

"You always dress like this for the nightshift?"

His frown slowly gave way and when he laughed, he was more handsome, more appealing than ever. She licked her lips and his gaze locked on her mouth. Her breath stalled in her lungs as he dipped his head, slowly closing in until his lips brushed across hers. Fleeting. There and gone and as soft as a butterfly's wing.

Holy cow. Her heart hammered. That wisp of barely-there contact sent her entire body into overdrive.

He watched her carefully. "That was probably—"

"A good start," she finished. "At least from this side." She reached out, curling her fingers into his T-shirt and stepping closer. No sweetness in the second kiss. The moment their lips met it was all hot demands and sultry promises. He nipped her bottom lip and a jolt of need burst low in her belly. She reveled in his taste, breathing him in deep, as his tongue twined with hers.

Oh, such a bad idea. A breach of protocol for sure. Patting his chest, she whispered. "Here comes the cavalry." In the blaze of headlights from an approaching vehicle, he looked as dazzled as she felt. It was immensely satisfying. "I won't keep you."

"I wouldn't mind if you did, Anna."

Whew, that look would keep her warm for the rest of her days. "Guess we'll discuss that later." She hopped up into the driver's seat, nearly moaned at the heat in his gaze.

"Do me a favor?" he asked, still holding on to her door.

"What's that?"

"Call me when you get back to your room."

He was so sweet. That need to shelter and protect obviously went bone deep. She had his personal cell number from when he'd dropped off the SUV for service. "I will."

"I'll be waiting." He closed her door and stepped back.

Slowly, she pulled away from the scene, telling her heart to cool it with the pirouettes. So she'd never felt her toes tingle quite like that. Just because the man could kiss didn't mean he should be kissing *her*.

Definitely not while she was pretending to be someone other than herself.

THEO WATCHED HER DRIVE OFF, willing his body under control. Anna's sweet taste lingered on his tongue, left him craving more. Later. Right now, he had a mess to clean up and it would be hours yet before he could get back to bed. Alone. He might as well write off sleep tonight. He checked his phone, even though it was way too soon for a call from Anna.

"You doing all right?" Cahill's voice was too low to be overheard.

Aw, hell. Had his deputy seen that kiss? He glanced back to the end of his driveway, hoping it hadn't been too obvious. At least he knew he wasn't stepping on the younger man's hopes and dreams. "Fine."

Pulling his head down from the clouds, he took in the people working the scene as if he was just another victim. But he wasn't. He was the authority who still had a drug seizure in his station, the officer who'd sent a body to the officials who would eventually make an identification. Though he would've denied the implication a week ago, it was becoming clear that he'd pissed off someone enough to make himself a target.

"How did she hear about this, ah, situation?" Cahill asked.

Theo shook his head. "She didn't. Said she was out for a drive, saw the emergency lights and stopped to offer help."

Cahill's brows shot up. "Quite a coincidence."

The reaction, the words, lit a fire under Theo's natural skepticism. "Suppose it is," he allowed. Once again, he faced uncomfortable doubts about all the things he didn't know about the newest arrival in Kite Creek. "She's former military," he reminded the deputy as well as himself. "Not easy to shake off that urge to run into a situation."

"Guess not."

He couldn't quite stop the niggling doubts. It was odd that she'd been driving out this way around the same time trouble had found him. That might've been the best kiss of his life, but he'd be smart to take a step back until he could definitely separate her from the criminals in his county.

FEELING MORE than a little guilty and wildly turned on, Anna chose to send a text rather than call when she reached her room safely. She didn't need Theo's smooth, mellow voice stirring her up any more. Somehow, his immediate text response made it challenging to get to sleep anyway.

Her dreams were peppered with tantalizing what-ifs about Theo and the sheets were tangled around her legs when her alarm sounded a few hours later. She dragged herself up and out of bed, making it to the garage on time.

A couple of locals filled her morning with minor concerns and one scheduled brake job, but it wasn't enough to erase the lingering effects of that kiss. Something about him drew her, made her wish for impossible things. They could hardly have a relationship on the false pretenses of her arrival in town.

If she couldn't tell him the truth, she needed to find a way to distance herself before one of them got hurt. She stewed on it all through the day, rehearsing what to say when she bumped into him at Patty's.

But he didn't go to the diner, in fact, his vehicle remained at the station all day. Deputies came and went. A crime scene van with the state police logo stayed for over an hour. She stuck with her routine, fighting an irrational disappointment over not seeing him.

It was crazy to be this jacked up over a kiss.

She stuck with her routine, spending much of the night watching over his place.

The next day his official vehicle didn't come into town at all. She'd heard, through Grandpa Cahill, that he was having a security system installed. Top of the line according to the chatter. A few hours later, Claudia confirmed the system was up and running.

At least she could stay in her motel room for the entirety of the night. It annoyed the hell out of her that the change actually made her a little sad.

The next day, she was helping Shane with his pet project when her phone chimed. It was the jingle she'd assigned to Claudia, so she ignored it until she had some privacy. During her walk up to

Patty's to grab food, she read the series of messages, the last one a link to a news article about a muscle car full of drugs found in the Big Bend National Park, right at the Texas-Mexico border. The vehicle had been abandoned and, so far, no one had found the driver. The car pictured was a similar make and model to the one that had nearly flattened Theo several days ago.

Anna had decided long ago that if anyone she cared about ever went missing, she'd want Claudia on the case. The woman was remarkable at unearthing the most revealing clues.

If the situation in Texas was tied to the situation up here, why were the drivers abandoning their haul? Was that just a relay exchange gone wrong?

She reviewed the earlier text messages that detailed what appeared to be a monthly drug relay through the Black Hills. Apparently, the area around Kite Creek was a stopover, but Claudia hadn't yet figured out why.

What would make a drug mule stop? Anna wondered. Time was money for suppliers and dealers. Yes, the fishing up here was a draw for sportsmen, but the average cartel driver wouldn't fit in with that crowd. Then again, arrest reports consistently proved that drug mules came in all shapes and sizes.

She'd driven the area frequently since her arrival to get familiar with the terrain and the landmarks so she could find Theo if anything went wrong. There weren't too many roads that tied in to the highway. Approaching from the north, wilderness crowded the highway until suddenly Kite Creek appeared. Same thing coming from the south. Nothing but stunning views and blacktop between here and Sturgis.

She sent a text back: Slow day here. I'll see if I can get time off and find a back road or spur that leads to a hideout.

It wouldn't be hard to get the afternoon off. She'd finished the only appointment on the schedule and Shane could take care of any emergencies.

Her phone rang with an incoming call from Claudia and Anna picked up, stopping down the street from Patty's so she could speak freely.

"I have two potential explanations," Claudia said, skipping any pleasantries. "One, there's a drug making operation right under the sheriff's nose. The drivers stop to pick up additional supply."

"Valid theory." Anna wished she could discuss this openly with Theo, but asking him would only blow her cover if she let loose with her inquisitive nature. "And two?"

"They're squatting somewhere and changing drivers to keep things rolling nonstop."

That made a lot of sense, too. Maybe the key to the relay was a team of drivers. One with the product and one to get the driver out of the area when the car was handed off.

"That could explain the wreck and the John Doe a couple weeks ago," Anna mused. "And it would sure explain how someone can be close enough to harass Theo or eventually make a grab for the drugs without being seen around town."

"Theo is it?" Claudia asked, humor and curiosity putting a spark in her voice.

Anna pressed her lips together. Claudia wasn't a gossip like the troublemakers in Anna's hometown, but it was hard to let go of the old defensiveness. "Everyone calls him Theo or Sheriff. Small town rules."

"Uh-huh."

"Stop." Anna laughed it off. "I know you've seen the pictures. The man is sexy as hell."

"Which brings me right back to your use of his first name."

Anna wasn't fooled by Claudia's prim tone. The woman wasn't the judgmental type. They were colleagues, friends really, but Anna would *not* kiss and tell. Nothing to tell anyway. Since that startling kiss the other night, she hadn't even seen him. Without the apps on her phone that kept her informed of any radio calls between the sheriff and deputies and shared his travels per the GPS tag, she'd be struggling to keep her bosses updated on his safety.

"I hadn't considered the idea of exchanging cars or drivers nearby," she said, getting her mind back on the job. "That changes the scope."

Her homework on the area and the threat to Theo, combined with this new theory from Claudia had her intuition prickling. "I need to find where they're hiding."

"You need to keep eyes on the sheriff," Claudia reminded her. "I can send in others to look for the drug crew."

"Right. I'm on track," Anna promised. "Have you confirmed what they're running?" It would help to know why they were hell-bent on taking out Theo. To her mind, the logical move was to lay low, but they'd made two direct attempts in less than a week. "Could it be there's something special about the cocaine he seized?"

In the background, Anna heard Claudia's fingers flying over her keyboard. "Those drugs are still at the station?"

"Yes, as far as I know."

"I'll look for any analysis from the seizure in Texas. They still haven't identified the John Doe your sheriff pulled from the trunk." Claudia's grumble was abruptly cut short with a merry laugh.

"You okay?"

"Yes. Baby girl is up. Her daddy is on the case," she assured Anna. "If I'm right about the timing, the relay could come through any day now," she warned. "Stay alert."

"Always." Anna ended the call, chuckling as she imagined Claudia and Nathan discussing dangerous cases while juggling dirty diapers and late-night feedings.

Smiling to herself, she resumed her walk to the diner only to see Theo coming out with a to-go bag and drink cup. Some undercover bodyguard, she completely missed him walking over. He must be grabbing lunch before heading out on his own circuit of the county.

Sure enough, he jogged back to the station and straight to his SUV.

Dang it. After the attempted attack at his place, she felt more compelled than ever to watch his six. She had to find a way to stay on his six.

Hank Patterson's instincts about the danger to Theo had been spot on. She wasn't about to let her bosses down. Plus, she liked Theo—and his kisses —too much to watch him get hurt simply because he thought he was invincible.

Well, maybe not that exactly, but the man was too independent for his own good. As evidenced by the recent near misses.

She picked up the food and hustled back to the garage to drop it off. "Do you mind if I head out early today?"

"Big plans?" Shane shot her a wink.

Yes, though it was probably a far cry from what he was thinking. "Not exactly," she hedged. "I just wanted to get out for a bit."

"You could do that and do me a favor if you're up for it. A delivery truck is waylaid down in Sturgis with the parts I need. Any chance you could run down and grab it for me?"

That would put her out on the road where she wanted to be, albeit some distance from Theo's usual circuit. "Any chance you'd let me take the Charger?"

The low-slung muscle car would make short work of the trip and get her back in the area much faster if something did go awry.

Shane rolled his eyes, but a second later he tossed her the keys.

Grinning like a kid on Christmas morning, she headed out. Sliding behind the wheel, she synced her phone to the car and then sent a text to Claudia, asking her to keep watch over Theo while she searched the area south of town.

Anna obeyed the speed limit on the way to Sturgis, though it was tempting to open it up and test both the engine and her skills on the road. Making quick work of picking up the parts Shane needed, she was back on the road within a few minutes.

Her heart lurched when Claudia's number interrupted the song she'd been singing along with.

Anna used the hands-free option to answer. "What's wrong?"

"Easy. Everything is all right with your sheriff," she said.

She took a good, deep breath, letting her heart rate settle. "I've asked you to stop that," Anna scolded with zero heat. She changed the subject. "Just for the record, I haven't seen any side roads that aren't clearly marked on the map already."

"If the sheriff wants to find where this crew is hiding, he needs a drone," Claudia murmured. "Let me see what I can do about that. In the meantime, don't you dare take any detours."

The motherly tone made Anna want to salute. "I promise to behave."

Claudia gave a theatrical sigh. "Be still my heart. With other protectors I know that's just talk. With you I can rest easy."

Anna wasn't so sure that was a compliment. Pushing the speed, not too much over the limit, she obeyed her intuition to get back to town. She was nearly back to Kite Creek when she saw the flashing lights in her rearview mirror.

She slowed down and turned on her signal, letting the officer know she intended to pull over, while she looked for a safe spot on the shoulder. A groan escaped her lips when she realized it was Theo who had pulled her over.

She knew the way his mind worked. New

woman in town, good with cars, shows up within a couple weeks of his shocking dead body and drug bust. She'd been nearby on two direct attack occasions. Hot kiss aside, if Theo didn't suspect her of being part of the problem in his town, she'd be disappointed in him.

Resting her hands in clear view on the steering wheel as he approached, she braced for the worst.

CHAPTER 6

Theo had been swearing under his breath from the moment the driver of the sleek, charcoal Charger had blown by him. The fool. Overconfident drivers were the bane of his existence.

Even at their worst, these situations were far better than the violence of his operations overseas. Still, every accident took him back to those twisted vehicles, the harsh smells of smoke and blood, the broken bodies and traumatic outcomes. He would do whatever it took to make this stop a memorable experience for this driver. With luck, a hefty fine would convince them to change their reckless ways.

He took a minute to run the plate, surprised when it came back registered to Shane. The owner of the garage loved his fast cars and bikes, but he was rarely so reckless on the road. And he wasn't in the habit of loaning his prized car to anyone who asked for the keys.

Inwardly, Theo groaned, having a pretty good idea who was behind the wheel as he walked up to the car. Sure enough, bending low to peer into the passenger side window she'd lowered, he met Anna's gaze. She'd removed her sunglasses, making it easy to read the uneasy guilt swimming in her big brown eyes.

"Hello, Sheriff."

"Anna." Disappointment coursed through him, along with a wariness that he'd mentally moved her into the accepted status far too quickly. Even before that kiss. "Do you know how fast you were going?"

"At the time I saw your lights I was twelve miles per hour over the posted limit," she replied without her usual smile.

He didn't care for her calm, or her accuracy, though he couldn't have said what response he would've preferred. "Do you have any weapons in the vehicle?"

"Yes, sir. A 9mm Beretta." She tipped her head to the glove box. "You can open it. Take a look."

He didn't want to do this, didn't want to face the doubts surging like a tsunami. Hell, he'd kissed this woman just a few nights ago. At least there was no one else out here to point out that he'd probably been duped. "Keep your hands on the wheel."

"Of course."

He opened the passenger door, then the glove box, and pulled out the gun. Standing back again, he checked the safety was on before tucking it into the back of his belt.

Her having a weapon wasn't necessarily a sign of guilt or bad intentions. It was a common choice in this area and in Anna's case, there was the additional factor of being fresh out of the Army.

Or so she'd said.

Theo jerked his mind away from that trap. He'd checked her record himself and while double-checking over the past few days, he hadn't found the first whiff of a falsehood in her background. He had friends who knew how to really pick apart the details on a person, especially those they tried to avoid or cover up. Maybe it was time to call in a favor or two.

She didn't seem the least bit annoyed with the stop, didn't show any sign that his avoiding her after that kiss bothered her. *That* rankled. He was annoyed as hell with all of it, primarily her careless speeding on these treacherous roads.

Maybe he needed to be crystal clear with her. About all of it, his doubts included. "Anna, I need your driver's license."

"Yes, sir. It's in a pocket on my phone." Again, she only used her chin to indicate the phone in the cupholder next to her seat. "Would you like me to hand it to you?"

"I can reach it." He had control of her gun and despite the misgivings running through his mind, he didn't think she would attack him. Hell, if she'd wanted to, she could've done so already. "Were you also on the phone while you were speeding?"

"No, sir. That wouldn't be safe."

Would she knock it off with the "sir"? He was only growing more agitated with her, himself, the entire mess. "Is that some kind of joke, Miss Lopez?"

"No, sir."

But he caught a twist of her mouth, as if she was fighting a smile. That was the last straw, either she was working with the crew trying to recover the drugs he's seized or she was a reckless driver who could've gotten herself killed out here.

"Damn it, Anna. What the hell are you doing?"

Her eyes went wide and her lips parted. Then she seemed to rethink whatever she'd been about to say. "Speeding. I'm sorry for it, but I assure you that's the extent of my misdeeds."

The part of him that had been hoping to kiss her again wanted to take that at face value. Desperately. Every time he'd seen her since, it was all he could do not to drop everything and go to her. For more kisses and whatever might come next. He'd been planning to ask her out on a real date, but this stop changed things.

He held up the Illinois driver's license. "I'll be right back."

"I'll be right here."

With a shake of his head, he stepped away from the vehicle. The Chicago address on her license matched what he'd already found on her. It was small comfort, but still a relief. He didn't find anything else incriminating, but he sat there for several minutes until he was sure he could be rational.

Nothing concrete tied her to the trouble in his town, except her unusual presence at two attacks on his person. Had she been sent in to distract him? Maybe she'd been so calm in those crises because she'd known they were setups all along. If so, the woman was the best actress he'd ever met in person, and he'd met a few, thanks to his friendship with Hank Patterson whose wife was a Hollywood A-lister.

If he hoped to get this straight in his head, he needed confirmation he could count on. Knowing what he had to do, he called Hank's office. Thankfully, he got the voicemail.

"Hey, Hank. This is Tannehill. You were right." The admission left a bitter taste in his mouth, but if he couldn't trust his instincts, Kite Creek and the surrounding county would pay the price. "I could use someone out here on my six," he continued. "And if possible, have Swede run a full background on this name, please." He read off the information from Anna's license. "She looks clean, but I'd like that verified by an outside source."

The timing of her arrival in his life had been too convenient to be ignored. Until he got a clean report from Swede, he'd keep his hopes for more kisses locked down and maintain a healthy distance from the beautiful, mysterious mechanic.

As soon as Theo returned her driver's license, he let her go with a heavy fine and a stern warning. Naturally, he'd kept her gun, promising to return it if she came into the station with her certificate to carry. She'd left the documentation in her truck.

She'd been an idiot, giving into the temptation to let loose with the Charger, but it had been glorious while it lasted. The car handled like a dream. As much as she wanted to reassure Theo that she had the training and experience to handle these roads like an expert, that would open the floodgates to more questions she couldn't answer today.

Maybe not ever.

Hard to enjoy the rest of her drive, knowing she'd singlehandedly screwed up her ability to do the one thing she was here to do. Staying close to Theo now would be a bigger challenge than ever.

It surprised her how much that hurt on a personal level. Maybe Claudia was right to imply that Anna was smitten with the sheriff. She stewed about it all the way back to the garage. Once Shane thanked her for the delivery, she gathered her keys and hopped up into her truck, synching her phone to her vehicle once again.

What now? Heading back to the motel was a coward's option. She couldn't just cruise up and down the main street hoping for a chance to set things straight with Theo. Minding the speed limit as if her life depended on it, she did a quick circuit of the area. His SUV wasn't at the station or his house. He was still out there doing his job and she would do hers, relying on the emergency dispatch app to keep tabs on him. Whether or not the sheriff trusted her, she would fulfill her professional responsibility.

Though she wasn't looking forward to the making the call, Claudia needed an update. Especially because she was sure Theo would soon be taking a harder look into her background. The story Claudia had built was ninety-five percent truth, they'd only scrubbed her Guardian Agency affiliation for this case. Still, better to be proactive and prevent any surprises.

As she cued up the hands-free option, an

incoming call came through from Claudia. Anna picked up right away. "Hello."

"Girl, what did you do? I was counting on you to behave."

Anna winced. "I got a speeding ticket while running an errand in my boss's souped-up muscle car."

Claudia snorted. "Has to be more than that. Tannehill isn't the kind of guy to freak over something that mundane."

When did he freak and how did Claudia know about it already? "Safety is important to him. He caught me pushing the speed limit out on the highway earlier."

"Could be he's more worried that you're pushing drugs."

She swallowed the groan. Of course, he was thinking she was part of the trouble plaguing him and his county. "I take it he's started digging into the background?"

Claudia cackled, the laughter seemingly out of her control. "Anna?" A man's voice came over the line. "This is Nathan. You might've broken my wife."

"Sorry about that. I have no idea what's so funny."

"I don't know all the ins and outs of your case, but according to the notes she's flapping her hand at, Tannehill called in a favor. Asked his pal Hank

Patterson to run a background check on you. Even went so far as to ask Hank to send someone to watch his back."

About time. Still, Anna wished for a black hole to open up so she could effectively disappear. This was so embarrassing. Patterson's team would never blow her cover, since they'd hired her to protect Theo in the first place, but she'd just smudged up the Guardian Agency's stellar reputation.

"Trust is fragile," she murmured. "Does that mean one of the Brotherhood Protectors will be showing up soon?" Naturally, she'd clear out, but not until she was sure someone capable was in town to keep Theo safe.

Claudia came back on the line. "Sorry. That was so unprofessional of me."

"Mm-hm. Must be going around."

"Ha. To answer your question, yes Tannehill asked Hank for backup. What he doesn't know is Hank has had one of his men on standby down in Sturgis."

"Good," she managed.

Why did that information sting so badly? She could be off the case by nightfall. If she was lucky, her bosses would wait for explanations until she was back in the Chicago office. Which was exactly where she belonged. Her shoulders cramped. This felt like so much more than a professional failure, like she'd missed a once in a lifetime opportunity with Theo.

Absurd.

She jerked her mind away from those thoughts. It wasn't as if they had any kind of future. "I'm going to finish my search for any access roads where this crew might be hiding out," she said. "Talk to you later."

"Hang on!" Claudia sounded as if she might climb through the phone. "Nathan will also be heading your way. He's bringing along a drone to help the search. Gamble has been in touch with the state police and a couple of federal agencies as well. Sounds like everyone is looking for any and all intel to break up this relay team. Whatever happens with Tannehill, your orders are to stay in Kite Creek and assist."

"Got it." She ended the call, hoping Claudia hadn't picked up on the emotions choking up her voice.

She was a Guardian Agency protector and good at her job. She would maintain her cover and her professionalism until this case was closed. And then she'd go back to what she knew and blend into the background of the city she adored.

It was a matter of due diligence, of giving hard data to whoever took control of Theo's safety, that had her heading north of town to continue her search. She'd marked three visible side roads to investigate on the return trip. Yes, that went against Claudia's advice, but she had to *do* something, anything to get this case back on track. Sitting on her hands while bullies of any stripe had their way wasn't her style.

The next highway sign indicated a major intersection in twenty more miles and she decided to turn back toward Kite Creek at that junction. Safer than pulling a U-turn on these roads in the late afternoon. Between the curving roads and the sudden shift from dusk to nightfall when the sun dropped over the mountain range, Theo had good reason to worry about drivers out here.

She refused to be one more statistic.

The app on her phone that was tuned to local emergency frequencies went off with a harsh series of beeps followed by the dispatcher's voice. Hearing the report of a fire at Shane's garage, Anna checked the roadway was clear in both directions and pulled that U-turn anyway. There was no time to waste. She stomped on the accelerator, applying all of her driving expertise as she guided the truck along the twisting roadway.

A bad feeling gathered in her gut and she tried to reason it away. Plenty of flammable materials in that garage. It could very well be a legitimate crisis. But her intuition screamed it was another setup. The crew had tried to run Theo down in front of the shop just days after her arrival. The sheriff's office was just up the street. The center of Kite Creek was compressed into a few blocks, which meant everyone would be distracted by the fire.

That would give this crew an opening to attack Theo or try and reclaim the drugs. They had to be squatting somewhere close to get in and out so easily without any one seeing them.

And she'd left him to fend for himself, when the threat had been clear. *Idiot.* She gripped the steering wheel, scolding herself over and over as volunteer firefighters called in on their way to the blaze. Tannehill chimed in that he was on the scene, along with both deputies.

She pushed, driving as fast as she dared until the welcome sign came into view. Her heart stalled between each burst of Theo's voice on the radio. No one passed her going the other direction. Good sign or bad?

Coming around the bend she saw the plume of smoke, black and dark, scarring the twilight sky. Swearing, she crept down the street, carefully aware of the distracted people crowding the sidewalks. Everyone's attention was on the fire.

Where else would they be looking?

Her pulse pounded in her ears. This was the perfect opportunity to take out Theo while no one was watching. She passed the motel on this end of town. The same family owned both places and she'd chatted them up enough to know no one from the drug relay crew was abusing their hospitality.

Following her intuition, she made two quick turns and zipped down the side streets until she could approach the garage from the opposite direction. As she suspected, Theo was in the center of the response, standing by as if he could will the firefighters to quick success. Anyone targeting him would have to go through a wall of bystanders.

The center of town was completely clogged due to the emergency, so she continued down the block and then turned up the hill toward the sheriff's station. If they couldn't get to Theo, the crew would likely go for the drugs.

Parking behind the grocery store, Anna used the loading dock for a bit of shelter from anyone who might be a lookout. Automatically, she reached for her weapon, only to remember she didn't have it. Well, there were other options. As quietly as possible, she left the cab and went around to the tool box in the truck bed, pulling out the tire iron. Moving as fast as she dared, she ran toward the station, her gaze searching the shadows for anything that didn't belong.

The light was fading and if the crisis down the street meant the station was unlocked, it would be easy picking for the crew who wanted to recover their seized shipment.

Near the far corner of the building, a motion-sensitive light spotlighted a person approaching the rear entrance. Anna froze, keeping watch. Male, though that observation was based mostly on the stride. The jeans were baggy and the hooded sweatshirt more so. The hood was pulled up, casting shadows over the person's face. She had no hope of getting a description unless she intervened directly. About the only accurate descriptor she could make was that he was less than six feet tall.

Mr. Hoodie went straight for the back door. The lock was electronic, she'd seen it herself on a prior recon. He fiddled with the lock a few times until, to her shock, the door gave and the burglar slipped inside.

Not cool. Her grip firm on the tire iron, she followed, scooting in before the door closed. Here in the back hallway, the only light came from the soft glow of the exit sign over the doorway.

Theo might've skimped on his personal security until forced to change things up, but even Claudia had been impressed with his security at the station. That lock had to be monitored and there were cameras in and around the station. She'd made a note of each one on her earlier visits. If she could get this guy's hood off, maybe they could make a positive ID that would connect him to the relay and the higher ups who were setting the schedule and calling the shots.

She followed the perp down the hallway to the

evidence locker. No doubt in her mind now. The fire was all about distraction and creating a window of opportunity.

Suddenly the lights flared.

In front of her, the burglar froze. Anna did the same.

"Looking for something?" Theo said, his voice low and menacing behind her.

The perp turned and, in the light, she noticed the stubble on his jaw. More importantly, she saw the gun in his hand and the leading edge of a tattoo at the inside of his wrist.

"Drop the weapon," Theo ordered.

She was sure he'd pulled his weapon as well. Caught in the middle, she cursed herself for making yet another mistake on this case. Watching the perp, trusting Theo not to shoot her, she saw Mr. Hoodie's finger move closer to the trigger. She swung out with the tire iron and knocked the gun from his hand before he could fire.

The would-be burglar howled and lunged. To take her down or get past her to Theo? Didn't matter. She ducked low and struck his knee with the tire iron, tripping him up and giving Theo room to decide what to do.

He didn't shoot, which she appreciated.

She kicked the fallen handgun into a side room and scrambled, pulling the door closed. When she turned, Theo and the perp were wrestling for control of his service weapon. Theo's reach was longer, but the perp was lightning-quick and clearly adept at playing dirty.

The two of them went down hard and Theo's gun clattered down the hallway. They were a blur of fists and elbows, rolling across the floor, each man determined to gain the upper hand.

Anna watched for an opening to help Theo, but they kept scrapping, slamming into furniture coming up hard against the tall desk that divided the front room. She couldn't just dive in without risking injury to the man in her protection.

Tires screeched to a stop out front and headlights flooded the front room. All three of them froze for a split second. Mr. Hoodie gained his feet and launched himself over the desk. Theo made a grab, but only caught the hoodie. With a duck and twist, the perp shook free of the fabric, limping to the door and out as fast as his battered legs could carry him.

Anna threw her tire iron. It caught the perp square in the back, between his shoulder blades. He yelped, but he kept going and with another squeal of rubber on asphalt she and Theo were alone in the trashed station.

"You okay?" she asked.

He didn't reply, his chest heaving. He had a scrape along one cheek and his knuckles were red from the punches he'd landed. She was sure he'd have a wealth of bruises by morning.

She resisted the urge to soothe him or offer advice on how best to ease the throbbing that would start soon. He didn't trust her. She started to clean up the mess, righting chairs and trash cans. Thankfully, only one computer was out here and at first glance, it seemed only the monitor had been damaged. Those were relatively easy to replace.

"Can you point me to a broom?" She kept her shoulders straight, her gaze level when all he did was glare daggers at her. He could doubt and question her as much as he wanted, she wasn't leaving until someone else showed up to watch his back.

"Hoping to clean up any incriminating evidence?" Theo closed the distance between them until he was toe to toe with her. "They left you behind. Why?"

Her chin dropped. He couldn't be serious. "Whatever theory you're mulling over," she said through clenched teeth, "I'm on *your* side."

"Maybe. I don't know you." He folded his arms and stared at her as though she were a bug under a microscope.

She took a careful breath. Losing her temper wouldn't convince him of her allegiance. She didn't have to put up with this. Although she couldn't let him out of her sight, she could keep tabs on him from a distance until Patterson's man arrived. By then, maybe Theo would be thinking clearly enough to talk sensibly.

"Regardless of what you think of me, I'm glad you're alive."

He pushed a hand through his hair, only rumpling it more. Bending to retrieve his hat, he dropped it on a desktop and turned away.

Was that supposed to be a sign of trust?

The lights came on, but his face was as stern as ever. "Did you set the fire at the garage?" His voice was as rough as gravel.

"No." She wished she could pick up the tire iron and leave, but that would only draw more attention to how she'd used it as a weapon. Judging by the look on his face, she was one wrong move away from him slapping cuffs on her and tossing her into the holding cell. "I wasn't in town when the fire started."

"Bet you know how to use a timer. Or maybe your pal started the fire so you could wait here to ambush me."

One of them had to be reasonable. Apparently, it would be her. "You're overwhelmed. Running on adrenaline. I'll forget you said that." He could clean up by himself. She started for the back door, eager to get away from him.

"Anna. Don't walk out of this crime scene."

She paused, throwing a look over her shoulder. "You know where I'm staying. If you need proof of my whereabouts at the time of the fire, I'll hand over the GPS report." He nodded and the fact that he needed to verify her story tore something loose inside her. Ridiculous, but true. "How is Shane?"

"Miserable. Anna—"

"This place was locked up tight." She spun around to face him, wanting a few answers of her own. "How did you get in here ahead of the thief?"

He was quiet for so long she'd nearly given up on an answer. Finally, in a low voice, he explained. "An alert was sent to my phone when an incorrect code was entered at the back door panel. I ran up here to head off trouble and opened the doors. If you're really on my side, explain how *you* got here."

"After what happened out at your place the other night..." She paused, unable to quell the memory of his mouth on hers. "I thought the fire might be a diversion. A way to empty the station so they could take back their drugs. The best way to get in unseen was the back door."

"Seems you were right." He scrubbed at his face. "Sorry I assumed the worst."

"I'm on your side," she repeated. "I get it. I'm a stranger." She stopped short of blowing her cover, though she knew he still wasn't entirely convinced. Surely by tomorrow, he'd have someone he could trust at his back. "You need to get Cahill and West up here to process the scene, check the video for a possible ID on that guy."

His gaze narrowed. "I know my job."

She held up her hands. "And you're good at it. Still, if the drugs are secure, it might be smart to get home and take care of yourself."

He gave a snort. "I'm fine." Reaching for his radio, he called his deputies back to the station. "First, we'll both give a statement. You'll turn over the GPS report. After that, we'll see."

She supposed that was better than him locking her up until his mood improved enough to hear reason.

CHAPTER 7

THEO'S BLOOD STILL POUNDED, anger and adrenaline a potent mix in his system as he drove from the station to his house at the western edge of town. There was a dull ache behind his eyes and his hands, ribs, and face were sore from the fight. The crew running these drugs through his county seemed damn sure he would roll over.

He'd left Cahill and West with the mess at the station. West was reviewing the video feeds in search of any and all angles that could be used for facial recognition of the intruder. Theo had confirmed Anna's story of how she'd wound up inside the station with the perp.

The only law she'd broken was the speed limit. It wasn't a crime to be new in town. Frustrated with himself for doubting her story, he returned her handgun. Then he'd gone a step further and invited her to his place for dinner. To his surprise, she'd agreed, trailing him to his place in her own truck. Now, at her insistence, they were walking the perimeter of his home for any signs of trouble.

"Take a breath." Anna aimed a flashlight around the basement windows. "We're almost done."

"They think I'm a putz," he groused.

Her bright laughter carried through the cool evening air. "Not anymore."

That was probably true. He confirmed the back door was secure and moved along.

"Why haven't you moved the drugs to the state lab?"

His hand flexed on his own flashlight as they returned to the driveway. "I failed the first time I tried it a few days after the seizure."

"What does that mean?"

He unlocked his door and entered his security code into the panel before the system got too loud. "It means someone was still in the area, watching and waiting for me to make that move." Closing the door behind her, he reset the system. "And somehow, they're still lurking around right under my nose."

He caught the way her fingers curled into her palms. "What happened when you reported that attempt?"

"We all agreed the drugs would stay at the station." He headed for the kitchen, hoping to divert this conversation with something more interesting. Like food. Or kisses. Probably too soon to hope for any serious affection after he'd written her a stiff fine for speeding and all but accused her of being a drug runner.

"Theo." She said his name as though it were a curse.

The tone made him want to smile, pretty much a miracle under the circumstances. "Look, I didn't want to put anyone else at risk."

"Hero complex."

"No." He'd seen that kind of thing first-hand during his SEAL days. "I'm aware of the boundaries of my ability and my position. No way was I putting the chain of custody at risk."

She was quiet as she followed him into the kitchen, giving him time for yet another replay of how she'd intervened when she should've stayed out of that confrontation at the station.

He removed his gun and locked it in the safe he kept in a kitchen cabinet. "You know, I didn't mention it, but the SUV has been running like a dream since you finished with it."

Her lips twitched as she watched him, but she didn't quite smile. "Happy to help." Her gaze dropped to his hands. "I'll gladly pitch in with dinner too."

"No, thanks." He shook his head. "I can handle it."

Her gaze tracked over his face and her lips parted. He knew he was a mess and spoke before she could. "You amaze me." Her eyes were calm as she watched him. He reached out and wiped a smudge of dirt from her cheek. Taking her hands in his, he stroked his thumbs over her palms, pleased when her breath hitched. "You saved my life."

Color crept into her cheeks. "You had it under control."

He wasn't so sure. His body wanted to run wild when it came to her. "Dinner." He'd promised to feed her. And surely, that would be a good first step in regaining her trust and hopefully her interest. "Then I'll take you back to the motel." Unless he could convince her to stay.

"Sure."

The shape of her lips on that lone syllable proved irresistible. Cradling her face, he lowered his mouth to hers. She rose up on her toes and met his kiss, her lips softer than silk. Just like the first time.

The kiss went from sweet to hot in moments, a rush of anticipation blazing through his veins. Her hands glided over his arms and around his neck. While he lived in the boonies, not a neighbor in sight, he wouldn't give the bad guys a show if they were watching his place. Hands on her hips, he guided her back toward the hallway so they weren't making out in front of the kitchen window.

Her tongue stroked over his, igniting a desire he didn't want to keep under wraps any more. To hell with taking things slow and being reasonable. "Anna, I don't want to stop."

"Good." Her hands tugged his shirt loose and slipped under the fabric to caress his skin. He moaned.

He pressed close, pinning her between his body and the wall, desperate to catch a deep breath. He wanted all of her right now. This frantic need had him by the throat, at war with the desire to savor each individual moment. He traced the shell of her ear with his tongue, smiling when her body shuddered. Kissing and nibbling his way down her throat, he smiled against her skin as her head fell back.

Suddenly she pushed at his chest and he backed off, hands out wide.

She grinned and yanked off her shirt, then brought his hands back to her waist.

For a moment he could only stare at the pale pink lace covering her breasts. Did she always wear something so feminine under her work clothes? This image would drive him crazy from now on.

He feathered kisses across the slopes of her breasts, breathing in sweet fragrance. She ran her hands through his hair, holding him close as he suckled the pebbled tips through the lace. She was so responsive, one amazing discovery after another as he stripped off her jeans and found a matching lace thong.

"Anna, you're killing me." He cupped the smooth flesh of her backside.

"I hope not," she said. "I'm not nearly done with you yet." She reached for his belt, but he stilled her hands.

She swore at him in Spanish and he laughed as he hit his knees. "May I?"

At her nod, her soft pleas, his mouth drifted over the supple skin of her midriff, down over her slender belly and trim thighs. He slid his fingers beneath the skimpy bit of lace and groaned. She was already wet. He teased her—teased them both —as he put his mouth to her core.

"Theo," she breathed.

He touched his tongue to her slick folds and her knees buckled. He caught her, nuzzled that sensitive juncture at her hip until she was steady. Standing, he swept her up and into his arms, heading toward his bedroom.

She pressed her lips to his neck, nipping lightly and he had to stop and take her mouth once more. Couldn't help himself. When they reached his room, he set her down at the edge of the bed and treated himself to a long, lingering kiss. Dragging himself away, he stripped off the rest of his clothing while she watched, her gaze molten.

She reached for the clasp of her bra and he

stilled her hands. "Let me." With a smile that made his own knees weak, she did.

"I haven't handled this well." He'd make it up to her, kiss by kiss, pleasure by pleasure. He couldn't explain how he'd become so attached so quickly. Maybe it was only physical, but as she arched into his touch, it didn't matter.

"Theo." Her husky voice was one more turn on. "I think you're doing just fine."

Losing himself in the soft fragrance of her heated skin, he indulged himself with hands and lips, learning every touch that made her gasp or sigh or—yes—press that sweet body closer to his. When the first orgasm hit, her body trembling under his mouth, she panted his name, pleading for more.

He couldn't deny her, or himself. She was glorious in her urgency, her eyes heavy with a passion that echoed the desire pounding through his system. Pausing to grab a condom from the nightstand and roll it over his erection, he took in the beauty of her in his bed, her hair a wild dark river over his pillow, her hands trailing over every part of him she could reach.

What had he done right to get this kind of lucky?

"Anna." He drove deep, buried himself in the hot, silky grasp of her body.

Her arms wrapped around him and she opened

her eyes, her gaze clouded with pleasure as he stroked in and out as slowly as he could. "Don't stop."

He had no intention of stopping. Bending his head, he captured her mouth in a searing kiss that left him seeing stars. There could never be enough of this. The heat, and tenderness, the potent connection that was perilously close to perfect.

Each time he sank deep he felt closer.

She tightened around him, her hips rising to match him. He felt her nearing the next peak, watched in awe as she cried out his name on another climax. She was glorious, her fingers digging into his shoulders. Thrusting deep one more time, he found his own shuddering release.

Breathless, her heart pounding under his, he forced himself to move. At her side, he stared up at the ceiling for just a minute while his body recovered. When he was sure his legs would hold, he got up and disposed of the condom.

Returning to the bed, he was struck again by the sight of her here, in his house. His room. Her supple body was pure temptation and he bent to kiss those rosy lips, his hand cruising over the curve of her hip, down her thigh.

Her eyelids fluttered open and she met his gaze. Trailing a finger over his jaw, it seemed the sexy smile dimmed just a little. "There's something you should know." She scooted to sit up, raking her hands through her hair.

He already knew he was the luckiest man alive, pleasured so thoroughly by the woman who'd saved his life twice now. She must be referring to something else, something he wasn't going to like if the guilt that flared in her deep brown eyes was any indication.

He stretched out on the bed, propping himself on his elbow. He reached for her hand, tracing her fingers. "Seems like you'd best spit it out."

"Probably so." She pressed her lips together and spoke to their joined hands. "I'm here on an assignment."

A chill slid down his spine, but he wouldn't jump to conclusions or assume the worst. Not yet. "I didn't realize being a mechanic worked that way."

"Don't be obtuse." She chewed on her lip, her gaze flicking to his and away again. "I was sent here. To Kite Creek. To *protect* you."

He stared, unable to make any sense of that statement.

"I'm a professional protector, usually a driver," she muttered. "And usually only called on for short-term gigs in the city." She tugged, trying to free her hand, but he didn't let go. "The security agency I work for was hired to send someone in to watch your back."

He felt as if she was talking to him through a long, dark tunnel. All the warmth he'd felt a minute ago vanished. What they'd just shared couldn't have been a stunt. The chats over pie, that first kiss… No. He wouldn't believe she'd faked all of that.

There was only one person he knew who cared enough to hire a covert bodyguard. He should've seen through her from the start. "They sent you."

Now her eyes met his, held. That serious, steady expression was back. "Yes."

"You're not former military?"

"I am." Her earnestness showed in the way her fingers tightened on his. "Just not as recently as I led you to believe."

Theo rolled out of the bed. "Hank Patterson." He caught the rant just in time. It wasn't her fault Hank was persistent. "He hired you for this."

He saw the moment his poor choice of words registered in a way he hadn't meant at all. Her eyes blazed and her cheeks flushed. She jumped up and he caught her before she could dash away or attack him.

"Wait. Wait! That's not what I meant." Desire stirred, having her in his arms, but if he kissed her now, he'd likely get slapped away. "I swear that was *not* at all what I meant."

The fight went out of her in an instant. "Why wouldn't you think it? My actions had to give you doubts, but I am a professional. I'm good at my job.

And—" Her mouth snapped shut, cutting off whatever she'd been ready to add.

That piqued his curiosity.

"You are." Things started to click into place. Her preventing him from being run down near the garage. Consistently running into her at Patty's. Getting to know the locals in much the same way he had done. Catching her speeding on the road when she must have been searching for the drug crew. Saving him from a bullet at the station. "You're a great bodyguard. Evidenced by the fact that I'm still breathing."

Her sharp chin lifted and her hands curled around his biceps. "Exactly. You *are* in danger, Theo. You needed someone on your six."

The truth hit him hard. He needed *her*, specifically, regardless of the dangers. But it was a little soon to be making declarations like that. So he kissed her instead, an automatic response to her distress and her proximity. Keeping her lips occupied was the only way he could prevent her from arguing. He eased back, resting his forehead to hers. Hard again, his body was ready to dive back into the bed for an encore. Could only hope she was willing.

"You're taking this well," she said, her palms caressing his shoulders.

"Damn right. You've saved my life a couple times over." He skimmed his hands along the dip of her waist, down over her backside and brought her in close. "I have a few ideas about how to say thank you."

"Gratitude sex isn't what I'm after."

His lips cruised over her throat. "Then we'll call it a celebration of life." Picking her up, he latched his mouth to hers, groaning in sweet anticipation as she wrapped her legs around his hips.

CHAPTER 8

AN HOUR LATER, Anna was sure she was glowing with a no-sun-required kind of blissful radiance. The man knew how to deliver when it came to pleasure. She was also starving.

Her stomach rumbled and Theo laughed, his warm, rough palm gliding over her midriff.

"Sounds like the adrenaline rush is over," he rolled closer, teasing a path across her bare shoulder, working up and over her collarbone until the stubble on his jaw a tantalizing rasp.

She arched into him and a soft moan slipped past her lips before she could stop herself. His breath tickled her skin as he chuckled, the sound low and enticing. "I'm not sure I have the energy to even help you cook," she admitted.

"I'll handle it."

She turned her head, getting lost in his deep brown eyes. "Take out?"

Not even that was as tempting as it should be. Patty's diner was fantastic, but it was also a drive. Anna missed the wide variety and easy availability of food in the city. Fresh sushi or some spicy Pad Thai would really hit the spot right now.

"Better," he promised. "Theo's homemade pizza."

Her stomach growled again and she was pretty sure it was giving up hope. Homemade pizza sounded like a long wait.

Grinning down at her, he kissed the spot between her eyebrows. "Trust me, honey. Thirty minutes and you'll be a believer."

She'd trusted him with the rest of her body, it seemed silly to worry about his ability to feed her. He rolled out of the bed and she admired the excellent view of his muscled back, butt, and legs. "You stay in shape," she murmured.

He shot her a smoldering look over his shoulder. "Same goes." He grabbed a clean pair of jeans and pulled them on, not bothering with underwear. "Worth every hour when you look at me like that."

Oh, no. She'd gone all girly on him. Fallen back into a second round of amazing sex minutes after revealing her true purpose in his town. Now, she was perched at the very edge of losing her heart to the man she should be focused on protecting.

"Theo. I should be clear. This isn't... that is..." She sat up, bringing the sheet with her to help combat this sudden burst of modesty. How to explain? She'd given him no reason to believe that this wasn't the way she normally worked.

He came over, bracing his hands on either side of her hips. "You don't need to say a word." He kissed her, firm and fast.

She traced his mouth with her fingers, wanting to give him the right words. "What happened between us is, *um*." Why couldn't she own this?

"Simply put we're combustible, Anna. And don't you dare reduce it to some post-fight adrenaline factor."

"No." Not that. She'd been intrigued by him since rolling into town, attracted before they wrapped up their first conversation in front of Patty's counter. A complete set up of course, but he'd surely come to that conclusion on his own by now.

"You don't seem mad about me being here undercover."

His eyes danced with mischief and he tugged the sheet down so he could kiss her breasts. "Not thrilled with this particular cover," he joked. "Any issue I have with Hank's sneaky approach I'll take up with him later. With you, I have zero complaints or concerns."

She ran a hand up and down his sculpted arm.

"That's good." She didn't have a single complaint about him either. Digging deep, she said what she should've said before falling back into bed with him. "This isn't my habit. Sleeping with a client," she said in a rush.

"You're saying I'm your first." The gleam in his eyes was absolutely wicked and more than a little possessive.

She pressed her lips together, unsure if she was amused or concerned about his response. "In a manner of speaking, yes."

He kissed her with such hot tenderness she marveled that she didn't melt away. When he eased back, his breath was soft against her cheek. "None of what happened between us undermines the way I see you," he said. "You've been the utmost professional. Shown uncompromising integrity. Beautiful badass." He punctuated each description with a kiss and then stood up. "Do what you need to do." His smile was devastating. "I'll be in the kitchen."

When he walked out, Anna scooted out of the bed and into the bathroom. She splashed water on her face and tried to take comfort in his words. She *was* a professional. They'd crossed a line, but few things in her life had ever felt as right as the moment her body joined with his.

Hooking up with a client wasn't her habit. In fact, she'd never been tempted to cross this line before. Theo was special, though she had no idea what to do with *that* new awareness.

She stared at her reflection. Really, she didn't need to do anything except keep him alive. At the moment she only felt like a woman high on the best sex of her life. She hadn't meant to get carried away, but she didn't regret giving in to the passions and sensual needs Theo stirred.

Once she'd freshened up, she pulled on jeans and her sleeveless top. Barefoot, she followed the savory scents to the kitchen.

Theo moved with ease around the kitchen from stove to counter and back again. Glancing up, he froze, his gaze tracking from her head to her bare toes.

"What?" He was staring at her so long, with so much intensity, it was all she could do not to fidget. "Something wrong?"

"No." He swallowed. "You're gorgeous and…" He cleared his throat. "You're hungry." His mouth firmed into a determined smile. "The crust is almost ready," he assured her. "Need a few minutes for toppings and then back in the oven to bake." He nudged the line of containers on the counter closer for her inspection.

She walked over, refusing to let whatever weirdness was happening keep growing. "Looks like plenty of options."

"I didn't know what you like on your pizza."

"Mushrooms and sausage and plenty of cheese." She eyed the offerings, including a pan of sauce simmering on the stove. "I really thought home-made was code for 'I unwrap it and bake it in my oven.'"

His brow flexed into a stern frown. "To keep the peace, I'll forget you just said that."

Hmm. This was an interesting, appealing side of him. She was tempted to tease a little more, but to keep the peace, she asked him about the whole process.

"Back in high school, my mom taught me how to make a pizza crust and sauce that can be frozen," Theo said. "I keep those stocked and then make sure I always have fresh cheese and other toppings on hand."

"Wow." Very impressive. "The sauce smells heavenly."

He opened a drawer and pulled out a spoon. "Come here." Dipping the spoon into the sauce, he held it out for her to taste. "Careful, it's hot."

Probably not as hot as the man holding the spoon. With her hand resting lightly on his, she blew across the sauce and then guided the spoon into her mouth. The perfect blend of spices warmed her all over and she closed her eyes in bliss. "My compliments to the chef," she said. "That is amazing."

"Thank you." His voice was a rough counterpoint to the smooth sauce.

The oven timer sounded and he pulled out the pan with the partially baked and oiled crust. As she watched, he built the pizza with mushrooms and sausage over the whole thing. On one half, he added black olives and onions. Then he covered it all in a blend of cheeses and popped it back into the oven.

"Can you wait 15 minutes?" he asked, setting the timer.

"For what might well be the best pizza of my life? Yes." She grinned as she helped him clean up and put containers back into the fridge. "You do realize that's no small praise from a woman who lives for Chicago-style deep dish?"

"It hadn't occurred to me." To her surprise, he closed the refrigerator and pulled her into his arms. "Good thing or I might've been nervous."

She rested her hands on his shoulders, let them drift down over his pecs. He felt so good. Warm. Solid. She wouldn't let anyone hurt him and she found herself wishing she could keep that vow beyond the current case.

Unsettled by the direction of her thoughts, Anna eased out of his embrace and helped him set the table. He offered her a beer as he poured one for himself, but she chose a glass of water. Technically, she was still on duty and expecting more information from Claudia any minute now.

Just when she thought she couldn't take the aromas of the baking pizza, the timer went off. Theo served them both and they sat down. She dug in, the hot cheese nearly burning the roof of her mouth, but it was so tasty. "Amazing," she repeated. "You could give Patty a run for her money."

"She asked for the recipe after hearing about it from Cahill and West. I had them out here when I moved in. But I have no intention of sharing. Besides, I like Jerry too much to put him out of business."

It took her a second to recall that Jerry was the owner of the Italian restaurant next to the motel on the south end of the main drag. "You are too kind. This would definitely shut him down." She couldn't imagine anyone wanting another kind of pizza after tasting Theo's. "Care to divulge the secrets of this crust?"

"Sourdough."

Sure he was joking, she looked up and discovered he was serious. "You are a man of many talents."

"I like to think so."

Which begged the question of why he was choosing to live up here where people only knew him as the sheriff. "You don't have to tell me, but I'd love to hear why you stay in Kite Creek."

"Hard to be the county sheriff from anywhere else."

"You know what I mean."

He'd taken a big bite of pizza, but she was willing to wait him out. Once he'd chewed and swallowed, and taken a long drink of beer, he narrowed his gaze at her.

She only blinked innocently.

His gaze dropped to his plate. "I like knowing who's around me." He rested his hands lightly on the table and took a deep slow breath. "My last deployment was basically an extended recon mission. We were looking for a few key people in markets crowded with unfamiliar faces. The air was thick with noise from motor bikes, animals, vendors and customers. It was all clashing sounds and colors."

He drained the rest of his beer and set the glass down carefully. "Suffice it to say, our mission didn't go smoothly. On the teams we like to think we're invincible. Hell, we need to believe it. But sometimes..."

"I understand." She waited until his gaze focused on hers once more. "No, I wasn't an operator like you, didn't see a fraction of what you saw, but my service wasn't all smooth roads. Sometimes no matter how well we know our job, someone has other plans that we can't anticipate."

He bobbed his chin. "You're right about that.

When I got back to the civilian world I struggled. Didn't matter that I was stateside, unfamiliar faces made me jumpy. That made it hard to sleep, hard to get perspective. And damn hard to live."

As much as she appreciated his candor, the story put an ache in her chest. "Not an uncommon situation."

"You're right. I tried support groups and a couple of recommended counselors. But it didn't improve. Even around my family or hanging out with members of my team, I couldn't stop looking for the threat. Or rather, seeing the threat in every face I didn't know. So I took off, searching for quiet."

"In a casino?"

He shook his head, a wry smile twisting his lips. "Should've known you would do the homework."

"Guardian Agency protectors go the extra mile," she teased.

He reached across the table and traced the edge of the ring on her index finger, then stroked her palm with his thumb. Her body heated at the touch. "The casino *was* an improvement. Weird, but true. Plenty of regulars, uniformed staff, easy to spot the tourists. And for a change, most of the loud sounds were usually happy endings."

She hadn't thought of it that way.

"I'd come up this way to fish on my days off," he continued. "Found the real quiet out in the water.

Got to know a few of the folks and they grew on me. The only thing I'd change is the perpetual temptation people have for speeding on those dangerous curves. I had no idea how many accidents our office would handle in a given year. Sometimes the damage is too familiar."

She understood that as well. Though she stayed in her seat, she wanted to soothe him until those dark shadows in his eyes faded away. "Will you run for re-election?"

"As long as they'll have me," he said. He leaned back in his chair. "The good up here outweighs the bad. Or it will as soon as these drug runners learn they can't cut through my county."

"I'd think it would be harder to be so invested in each and every individual." Knowing every person had some obvious advantages, but the sense of responsibility that came with it was a big downside for her.

"No situation is perfect." He reached for her hands again, as if he couldn't get enough contact. "For me, it's better than wondering what some random stranger will do next."

She understood his point of view, mainly because she was exactly the opposite. "Kite Creek is beautiful," she began. "And the people have been welcoming. My previous experience in small towns wasn't that way at all."

He cocked an eyebrow and suddenly she was

spilling her guts. "I grew up in the smallest of small towns in Texas." Now she wanted a beer more than ever, but she would not allow anything to impair her reaction time. "Everyone knew everyone, all right. And they all seemed to excel at judgment." If she pressed hard enough, she could still feel the ache of her bruised pride somewhere in the vicinity of her heart. "No one had much hope for me, spending all my time in a garage with a bunch of men." She studied the ring on her finger. "My mom gave me this on my fifteenth birthday. It's tradition." On a laugh, she explained. "It only comes off when I'm working in the garage."

"I noticed," Theo said.

The comment sent a warm pulse through her system. "I think my mom hoped it would tame my wild side."

"No luck?"

"Not really," she admitted. "I love wearing this connection to the amazing and strong women in my family, but no one back home would ever have seen me as more than the bad-attitude tomboy. Without the Army, a chance to follow my interests and make something of myself, I'd probably be stuck and miserable."

"Why'd you leave the Army?"

She cringed dramatically and gave his hands a squeeze before pulling back. "Well," she drew out the word. "It was recommended that I find a new career after butting heads with an officer who didn't believe women could or should handle machines."

"He wanted you to handle him?"

She winced. "That obvious?"

Those days were behind her and she rarely let it show how much it bothered her that a bully had dictated her path. Thankfully, she'd reported that officer and still landed on her feet with the Guardian Agency. Since then, she'd never once had to worry that her intuition or instincts would be overruled solely because she was female.

"No, it's not obvious, but I came across my share of jerks while I was serving my country."

"They're everywhere."

He glanced around. "I hope not."

"Definitely not in this room," she said with a smile. Getting up, she went to his side of the table, laughing as he pulled her into his lap for a long, steamy kiss.

Her phone chimed and seeing Claudia's number on the display was as effective as a cold shower. "Text from my tech support," she said. "My boss and your friends are sending in backup."

He frowned just a little. "Probably smart."

"I agree. This drug relay crew is getting bolder and I'd rather not play roulette with keeping you safe while we track down where they're hiding."

"It's my job to take the big risks." He stroked a

hand up and down her spine.

She shifted away from his touch before she lost her focus entirely. The last thing they needed was for him to pull out the independent sheriff routine. Leading by example, she said, "Everyone reaches a point where they need to lean in and accept the offered help. This is your point, Sheriff."

He snorted.

"I mean it." Her phone rang. "Behave or I won't put this on speaker."

He held up his hands in surrender.

"Hey Claudia, you're on speaker. I'm here with Sheriff Tannehill." She ignored the way his eyebrows arched over that introduction. Did he expect her to admit they'd just slept together?

"Hi, Anna. Nice to meet you, Sheriff," Claudia said, a smile in her voice. "Nathan, another Guardian Agency protector, will reach Kite Creek tonight. We have mounting evidence that the crew running drugs has a relay system in place. Certain drivers handle a section of the route. The plan is for Nathan to use a drone and see if he can find where the crew exchanges vehicles, drugs, or drivers."

That sounded like a solid strategy to her and Theo nodded his approval. "You'll be okay with the single mom thing?" Anna asked.

"We'll find out," she said on a small laugh. "He was the closest protector available and based on the timetables I've been putting together, we need to move quickly over the next day or two, or it will be another month before we can interrupt the supply chain."

"Understood." Anna realized she wouldn't mind spending more time with Theo, small town or not.

"In the meantime, I'm continuing my investigation of property records and building a search grid based on the encounters you've had, Sheriff Tannehill."

"Thanks," Theo said, his gaze intense on Anna. "Wherever they're hiding or making exchanges, they aren't creating enough of a stir to upset the folks nearby."

"If anyone can find a paper trail, Claudia can," Anna promised.

"Thanks for the confidence," the researcher replied. "I'll keep you updated on Nathan's progress, just sit tight and stay sharp."

"Thanks for the assist," Anna said. "Give that baby a kiss from me."

On a happy laugh, Claudia ended the call.

A text message came through almost immediately. "She says Nathan just passed Sturgis. I guess we have about an hour or so."

They cleaned up the kitchen and went out to the deck while they waited. The air was cool and Theo was hot as he drew her back against his chest. So strange to feel so close to a man she'd just met. It would be a challenge leaving him and his town behind when it was time to go. She couldn't be in love, that was just silly. Covering his bigger hands with hers where they rested on her midriff, she tried to find her perspective. She cared about his wellbeing as a client. At most he was a new friend with fabulous benefits.

He gave her a little squeeze. "What are you thinking about?"

You. She trembled at the tender brush of his lips over her ear. "You have so many stars out here," she said, afraid to address her rush of emotions. "Too much light pollution in Chicago."

"What about your hometown?"

"I don't remember it looking like this."

"Must be the mountains."

She turned in the circle of his arms and kissed him soundly.

"What's that for?"

"When Nathan gets here, I should probably avoid that kind of affectionate demonstration and I wanted to fuel my fix."

"You're hooked on me, huh?" His smile was full of promises she wanted so desperately to claim.

"That's one way to put it." She heard an engine on the road and jumped back, riddled with foolish guilt. It wasn't as if anyone could see them. "Nathan's here." Fishing her phone from her pocket she groaned. "I missed the text."

"Relax." Theo tapped his nose to hers. "We've got this."

And still, it felt like a connection she needed had been severed when he released her and walked out front. She trailed after him, trying to ignore the chill skimming down her spine.

A white SUV pulled into the drive and parked. Nathan emerged from the driver's side with a smile. A big, burly man Anna hadn't met climbed out of the passenger side.

Within minutes introductions were made between Nathan and Theo. In turn, Theo introduced Anna to the newcomer, Bear, one of Hank Patterson's Brotherhood Protectors. Apparently, Bear hadn't been on the same SEAL team as Theo when they were operators, but they'd met when Theo had visited Hank in Montana. Leaving the equipment in the car, the four of them went inside to review the situation and make a plan.

"You're taking it well," Nathan observed later, catching Anna in the kitchen while Bear and Theo chatted in his great room.

"What do you mean?"

"I expected more pushback when I heard we were backing you up."

"It's a good thing, believe me." She didn't feel the least bit slighted to have backup. "The crew is getting bolder. You heard about the attempt to recover the drugs Theo seized?" At his nod, she continued. "Theo's deputies are top notch, but three of them are no match for cartel drivers determined to make an example of the sheriff who got in their way. Besides, I'm used to team assignments in the city. Usually I'm the driver, extra eyes, or whatever."

"And I'm used to being the only protector on scene." He smiled a little. "With Claudia in my ear, of course."

"Of course." Anna shook her head. "You like being a dad?"

Nathan's eyes filled with pride. "She's a beauty and is completely the boss of us. If I start on the baby pictures, I might not stop for a year."

"Bring it," she said, laughing. Anna crooned over each and every sweet photo Nathan shared from his cell phone. "I'm happy for you both." She'd never given much thought to having a family of her own. Her siblings had enough kids to satisfy her rare bouts of baby fever.

Her gaze drifted across the room to Theo and she suddenly had an image of little ones with his eyes and stubborn independent streak. Her heart cramped.

Nathan tilted his head. "You and the sheriff, huh?"

"What? No." Her brisk denial left a bad taste in her mouth. "We just look close because it's his house. You could say we bonded during the fight earlier." She was more than close already, though she wasn't foolish enough to believe this interlude could grow into anything permanent. "You know how it is."

"Uh-huh."

He hadn't even used real words and she felt overexposed. "Stop." She lowered her voice, "He's a great guy. Completely dedicated to his work right here." Just like she was dedicated to her work in Chicago.

Sensing Theo's approach, she turned to the refrigerator and pulled out a couple of longneck bottles of beer. "Who needs another?"

As Theo accepted the offered beer, she caught the shadows in his gaze. He'd overheard her comment. So what? It was a compliment. With an effort she shut down the urge to say something in her defense. If he brought it up later when they were alone, she could make him understand. She loved his commitment and admired his grit and determination.

In fact, she was starting to love too many things about Sheriff Theo Tannehill. And if she dwelled on it, those factors would be a distraction. He was the best man she'd met in years. They were great in bed and out.

And as soon as he was safe, she would return to the city.

Alone.

CHAPTER 9

He's completely dedicated. A great guy. Theo kept hearing those words in Anna's voice. Hearing a hint of an excuse in her tone. As if being great and dedicated to the job was a problem. Hardly. A negligent sheriff would be a drug runner's dream. *Like his predecessor.* The old, corrupt sheriff had likely been a factor when this crew was planning their route.

He knew she appreciated his work ethic. Admired it. If this situation was any indicator, she worked her cases with the same "dedication". Hell, last night, Bear had handed him a thumb drive with her full history and a hearty chuckle. Apparently, Hank's company had worked in tandem with Anna's on several occasions and with a high rate of success.

So why did her assessment feel like needles jabbing under his skin?

He should just ask. The worst-case scenario would be an answer he didn't want to hear. Something along the lines of what happens in Kite Creek stays in Kite Creek.

Since that first kiss, before really, he was one hundred percent certain he wanted her to stay. Now that he knew her better, despite her pushing the speed limit, he was sure he wanted her to stay with *him*.

Last night, after Nathan and Bear had left for the motel, he'd drawn her into an embrace that ended with more amazing sex in his bed. They'd fallen asleep in a tangle. She'd been up and out of bed long before his alarm had gone off. It was easier to forgive her absence when he found her in the kitchen making omelets.

Over breakfast they'd agreed that she'd spend the morning at the garage, giving him room to bring his deputies up to speed without an actual bodyguard standing behind him. He had paperwork to keep him occupied, but his mind kept drifting to her down at the garage. The kid who'd broken in yesterday had to know who she was. What if they made an attempt on her?

He managed to send only one text message to check in and when she walked into the station just after noon, her hair pulled up into a ponytail and a smudge of grease on her chin, his relief was palpable.

The plan was for her to hang around, ready to ride with him as his bodyguard, if Nathan and Bear found anything with the drone search. Unfortunately, having her so close and having to keep his hands to himself proved to be a serious challenge.

"You don't need to watch me every minute," Theo said. He couldn't concentrate, though she wasn't doing anything intrusive. He was simply too aware of her, too aware that she was putting herself in harm's way for him. Maybe it was chauvinistic or outdated thinking, but every fiber of his being clamored that he should be protecting *her*.

"Get used to it." She winked at him. "You're the best view in the office."

Her knowing tone sent a jolt through him. Whatever he'd told himself about temporary arrangements and inescapable attractions, he wasn't buying it. There was far more than lust involved when he looked at her. More than he could afford to dwell on right now while dangerous criminals were exploiting his rural county and small law enforcement team.

"Flattery will not get you where you want to be," he said at last.

"Are you sure?" There was a wicked gleam in her eyes. "I think I could flatter you into an enjoyable mutual distraction if I put my mind to it." She hadn't moved an inch, but in his mind, he had her stretched out across his desk, her body an open invitation to pleasure.

"I have work to do." Except there wasn't anything going on. As a precaution, his deputies were handling the patrols. Another piece that didn't sit quite right. All his life he'd led by example. Sitting here, waiting for the scanner to squawk, was torture.

"It's natural to want to be out there."

He looked up and caught her soft, knowing smile. "Theo, come on. You're not my first client. Not even the first to go a little stir crazy while under protection."

He wasn't sure how he felt about that. Oh, he knew sleeping with the client wasn't her typical behavior. What had she called herself last night when she'd met Bear? The Guardian Agency's best short-shift guard. And she'd made it clear that she preferred cities over small towns. With good reason, but still.

He was more than attracted to her. He was attached to the woman who resisted attachments. If he wanted something lasting—and he couldn't deny his desire for more time with her—one of them would have to bend.

This was not the time to get twisted up with personal stuff. He needed to get his head on straight, stay focused on eradicating this crew once and for all. For those under his protection as well as for himself.

"Want me to order some lunch?" she offered.

"Sure." He was a little put off by her obvious control and patience.

He tried, and failed, to review a law enforcement journal while Anna paced back and forth as she ordered two daily specials and a couple of iced teas from Patty's. After having her in his arms, sleeping with her through the night, every move she made was more enticing, and kept him on edge.

Despite her teasing, he knew she wouldn't actually jump him here in the station. His loss, he thought as his gaze locked onto the sway of her hips. He scrubbed at his face, determined to focus.

Why hadn't Nathan checked in? Theo could—and should—lose his job if two civilians got injured, or worse, trying to gather intel for this case.

He stood up suddenly, grabbing a radio and his keys.

"Hold on there." Anna stepped in front of him, her hands resting lightly on his chest. "I didn't hear a call. Where are you headed?"

It was as if all his senses were dialed into that one point of contact. "Nathan hasn't checked in," he said, his voice gruff.

"He's a big boy and Bear is with him."

"Anna, this is a serious mess. I'm grateful you're

here watching over me. Hank was right that I needed the help, but I can't let anyone else do what I promised this county I would do."

"What you've done is bring in experts at a time of crisis. No way the three of you could handle this alone."

The truth stung. Without Anna saving him twice now, it would've been just Cahill and West trying to deal with this. "So how is it the two of them can manage?" he demanded.

Her eyes went wide and he was instantly shamed by his unreasonable outburst. Backing off, he apologized. "Sorry. That was inexcusable."

"That was *real*," she countered, nudging him back toward his desk. "Don't worry about it."

"You cannot be this forgiving." He sank back into his chair. "It's not natural."

"Let's just say I can read you. You're stressed, and rightly so. Nathan and Bear aren't really alone. They have the best oversight in the business. Claudia won't let anything happen to them."

Again, his role was to protect and serve, but he managed to keep his mouth closed this time. "This isn't an urban hub with cameras on every corner and storefront," he pointed out.

Anna perched on the corner of his desk and he covered her knee with his hand. Couldn't resist. "I wouldn't be surprised if she redirected satellites to cover them," Anna teased. "She had mama bear tendencies long before she became a mother." She leaned close and brushed her lips across his cheek. "Trust us," she said softly against his skin. "We've got this."

"Helloooo?" A voice called from the reception room. "Anyone home?"

Anna shifted to stand and Theo jumped out of his chair. "What's Patty doing here?"

Anna smiled. "Delivery."

He stopped short. "You're kidding. She doesn't deliver."

"Come see for yourself," Anna said over her shoulder as she strolled out to the main room.

Sure enough, Patty had come bearing food. This, more than anything else, proved Anna was one in a million. Though he remained on alert for any distress calls, he managed to devour the food and feel better for it.

Anna didn't try to keep a running conversation and somehow the silence was more intimate, more comfortable. A drop of Patty's secret sauce dotted her lush lower lip and he reached over and wiped it away with his thumb. Then, with Anna's eyes on him, he licked his thumb clean.

For a moment, he prayed they never resolved this case and she stayed in Kite Creek, his personal bodyguard and lover for the rest of his days.

That wasn't exactly the right attitude.

"Dessert?" she asked, her eyes bright. "I ordered the cobbler."

"I'm, ah, not ready for dessert." At least not cobbler. He'd eagerly have a taste of her, if she was offering.

"No worries." Grinning, she picked up the two small boxes loaded with Patty's popular triple berry cobbler and headed toward the kitchenette. "I didn't want to push my luck asking for a second delivery later this afternoon."

Following her, he leaned against the door while she stowed the treats in the fridge. "Patty's no pushover." He was about to say more when Anna's phone rang. He hoped like hell this was something they could act on.

She pulled it from her pocket. "Claudia," she explained as she answered.

Theo felt the adrenaline surge through his system. "On speaker."

With a nod, Anna did just that. "You're on speaker," she said.

"Good," Claudia said. "Hi, Sheriff. Nathan just confirmed he's found the likely relay point. He and Bear are headed back to town now."

"They're safe?"

"Absolutely undetected, just the way we like it. He'll have a full report shortly."

Theo had more questions, but Anna stilled him

with a hand on his arm. "Thanks, Claudia. I'll let you know when we have a plan."

"Good hunting," Claudia said. "I'm still working with some old pals, keeping watch for the next run to start."

For a moment after the call ended, they stared at each other over her cell phone. "We're close," she said. "When Nathan and Bear get here we can make a plan to intercept the drug relay. Your ordeal is almost over." The smile on her face was tight and a protest coiled in his gut.

Anna wasn't an ordeal. Of course, that wasn't what she meant. She was talking about being under attack, having his safety and his peaceful county jeopardized by criminals.

"Anna—" He didn't want this to be over, but he didn't know how to ask her to stay. She didn't care for the fishbowl tendencies of small town life and he couldn't go back to a city full of strangers. He needed to know, and trust, the people around him.

But how was he going to manage without her? Already he was hooked on her smile, her wry humor and her cool confidence. She'd be an asset to his department, but he was fully staffed. While she enjoyed the work down at Shane's garage, she was made for bigger challenges.

Bottom line, he didn't have anything to offer that would be worth turning her life upside down. That stung more than he wanted to admit.

"Here they are," she said, scooting around him.

He followed her gaze to the window overlooking the street and saw Bear behind the wheel as he parked the SUV. In the passenger seat, Nathan was on the phone. Judging by the man's soft expression, he was talking with his wife.

Family wasn't something Theo had contemplated in a long while, but as Anna moved forward to welcome the others, he thought about *her* as the family he wanted more than any other. He was being a fool.

"Sheriff," Nathan said after he'd greeted Anna. "I figured you'd want to see this as close to firsthand as possible."

"This way." The station didn't have a ton of bells and whistles but the monitor in his office was the largest after yesterday's fight took out the monitor on the desk out front.

Within minutes, Nathan had uploaded the video from the drone. "Your information was a big help," Bear said. "We worked our way north of town from where you found that body in the trunk."

Theo listened to the men report that the first two stops hadn't panned out. "I spent a few minutes searching the other side of the creek, but as you said, Anna, the terrain was too rough for muscle cars."

"Not much better where we found them," Bear said. "Where we think we found them anyway."

Theo studied the drone video. The images gave him a clear view of the entire layout of a property he hadn't seen in person. At one time it must have been gorgeous. Now, the two-story house and barn were run down, as neglected as the weed-filled yard in between the structures. One access road was nearly overgrown and relatively invisible from the highway. A second access road was a quarter mile to the north and wound through a stand of trees, eventually connecting straight to the ramshackle barn.

"I drove up and down the highway while Nathan was on the drone," Bear said. "This is an ideal location. While you have plenty of open land around here, nothing else is quite so convenient."

"My jurisdiction," Theo said, through ground teeth. "No wonder no one has called it in."

The property was surrounded by a thick tree line on all sides, enough to muffle any noises of vehicles coming or going.

Theo was furious that they'd used a place so close to Kite Creek for this nasty business. They had to stop it before someone got seriously hurt.

"This isn't your fault," Anna reminded him gently.

Somehow her understanding only made him feel worse. He sat down at his desk and looked up the owner of record. "I disagree. They're running drugs right under my nose," he grumbled. "The new sheriff is too lazy or ignorant to notice."

"You noticed," she insisted. "You seized product and made yourself a target," she reminded him. "Now we can make a plan. First, we'll interrupt the relay. In a best-case scenario one of these drivers will flip on the network and make a serious dent in the operation."

He hoped she was right. His email chimed. "Claudia." He opened the message and sat back. "She says the current owner of record is Abe Coffey."

"What the hell?" Anna exclaimed.

"You know him?" Nathan asked.

"Yeah." Her lips flattened and her gaze turned hard. She was beyond angry. "He hired some gang enforcers in an attempt to take out Billie Hamilton while she was the U.S. Attorney in Montana. If he's the owner of record, then he's been dipping into more crime than we thought."

"Still have to tie him to the operation," Theo pointed out. "Just because he owns the place, doesn't mean he's in on it. Easy enough to claim ignorance of anyone using the land."

"Leave that to Claudia," Nathan said. "If there's a connection, she'll find it."

"What now?" Bear asked.

Theo looked around, his gaze catching Anna's.

He knew they were thinking the same thing. "Now, I want to see it for myself."

"Probably better if we study first and make a plan," Anna suggested. "Once we know the relay is on the road we can be ready to intercept."

She was right. Going out too soon could prevent a clean capture. Or worse, put her and others at risk. "All right," he agreed. "Let's do this the smart way."

CHAPTER 10

SEVERAL DAYS LATER, behind the wheel of Theo's official SUV, Anna drove north, away from Kite Creek. They were headed to the property Nathan had located. According to the schedule Claudia had pieced together with help from her network of associates in other agencies, those drugs were moving today, tomorrow at the latest.

Theo had tried to protest her as his driver, but after reading the full report Bear had delivered, he'd relented. Or been outvoted. It depended on your point of view, she supposed. Regardless, she was his best bet at surviving any ordeal on the road.

"I was too close and didn't know it," Theo grumbled, his gaze on the terrain.

He'd been understandably annoyed from the moment Nathan had located the likely hideout.

She ignored the shiver that skipped down her spine. If he'd found this place on his own, he might've been killed before she had a chance to meet him. Before she had a chance to fall in love. It was highly unlikely they had a future, but it was nice to discover she had the capacity for intimacy—emotional as well as physical.

"Better that you're going in with someone watching your back," she reminded him.

Slowing for the turn, she kept an eye out for any sort of trap. The SUV muscled through the overgrowth hiding the first drive. Branches and leaves dragged along the roof and sides of the vehicle as she inched along.

They hadn't gone fifty yards when they reached a sunny clearing. A change they wouldn't have expected without the drone search. Anna squinted against the glare and slowed to a crawl.

"I'll be damned," Theo muttered.

She aimed with her chin. "Lots of tracks through here."

"Yup."

"Is Cahill in position at the secondary access road?" She waited while Theo received confirmation from his deputy over the radio.

"Let's move in." He dropped his sunglasses over his eyes.

With a nod, she did just that, pulling off the driveway to preserve any possible evidence for the crime lab about the vehicles moving in and out of this location.

From this approach, they could only see the house, not the barn set about a hundred yards behind it.

"Remember that cellar entrance immediately behind the house," Theo said. "Perfect place for an ambush."

"I'll stay alert."

"Park here while I look around."

"Not a chance, hot shot." He was *not* trying to treat her like some shrinking violet now, after everything they'd been through. "Have you forgotten my real purpose here?"

"Anna."

She held up her hand. "Don't start with me about civilians and safety. I'm here as your body-guard, not your girlfriend." *Whoops*. They might be sleeping together but no declarations had been made.

"Girlfriend?" He stared at her. "That's how you see us?"

"Yes." No point in denying it and this wasn't the time to debate it. "I'm attached to you. Personally."

"Anna, I—"

The change in his tone put her on high alert. Higher than she already was during the search for this drug running relay. "We have to table this, Sheriff. We have bad guys to catch."

His jaw firmed and he nodded once. "Let's go."

Thankfully, he didn't try to leave her behind again.

Guns drawn, they moved toward the house, Theo in the lead. Not her preference, but he wore his bulletproof vest and he *was* the officer in charge. This wasn't just another protector order, she was here to protect a law enforcement officer, so the normal approach had to be adjusted.

"Sheriff's department!" he called from the base of the stairs leading to the porch.

No one answered. They moved to the door and he paused to call out once more. He tested the front door and it swung open. They searched the small house, finding signs of recent habitation, but no one seemed to be home now. Had they changed the timeline?

"They haven't been gone long." Theo pointed to a cooler and a bottle of water. "Still has ice."

"We must've missed monitors on the driveway." Anna frowned as she peered out the windows. "They didn't pass us on the road." She'd been braced for that, ready to fulfill her role as his protector and his driver whether he liked it or not. "What now?"

He nudged aside the thin curtain at the back door and studied the barn. "We keep looking. There was hard rain two nights ago. Those tracks on the drive were fresh."

"Agreed."

He opened the back door to a hail of bullets. She yanked him back and he kicked the door shut.

Pressed to the floor, he had the audacity to grin at her when the shooting stopped. "I think you like throwing me down."

"Maybe a little. It's keeping you alive," she pointed out.

"True." He paused, listening to the continued silence. "Let's go out the front and circle around through the trees."

Three more gunshots were followed by a loud hiss. "That's the radiator," she said. "They shot up your SUV."

Theo swore.

Heavy engines roared to life. "We have to get out there," Theo popped to his feet and went straight out the bullet-perforated back door.

Muttering an oath of her own, she stuck to his heels as he raced toward the barn.

He charged right through the door and shouted over the sound of cars idling, "Sheriff department! Lower your weapons."

She came up beside him only to see the odds were completely level. Two against two, all of them armed. Just behind the men were two muscle cars, running and ready to go. She and Theo probably had more ammunition at the moment, but it was a disaster waiting to happen.

"Lower your weapons," Theo repeated.

She marveled at his even tone, the cool resolve on his face.

"We're just protecting our property," the taller of the two men said. "You're trespassing."

Anna recognized him from the short list of drivers Claudia and her network had identified on a previous leg of the relay. His haircut screamed money, the frosted tips of his dark hair styled to messy perfection. The zippered jacket and skinny jeans along with the latest high tops confirmed the general suspicion that he was still in college. At the very least, the confident swagger and fashion choices would make it easier to recruit drivers from the collegiate crowd.

As cool as Frosty was, the second young man was sweating profusely, his face red under his blonde hair. "What now, man?"

"Go. They won't shoot."

"Guess we know who's in charge," Theo said to Anna. "I recommend you stay," he countered. "Cooperate with us and this will go much easier for you both."

"This wasn't the deal, man." Blondie was panicking. "I-I can't go to jail."

"You won't," Frosty snarled. "Do the job you were hired to do. Go."

Frosty was backing toward the second vehicle, still staring at them over the barrel of his gun.

When Blondie dropped his weapon and reached for the door handle of his car, Frosty fired two rounds into his back.

Theo and Anna fired at Frosty, but they were a fraction of a second too late. The man had dropped into the driver's seat and was already pulling away. They only nicked his side mirror.

Theo rushed forward, checking for a pulse on the downed man. "He's gone."

"Call it in from the car." Though her heart hurt over the murder, she stepped over the body and slid into the driver's seat. "We have to catch him." If they didn't move fast they could lose Frosty. He was now their best hope of upending the operation. "Come on, Theo. He's not heading for Cahill. Get in!"

WHAT CHOICE DID HE HAVE? If they lost this driver on the drug relay route, the whole thing would be a bust. He jumped in and fastened his seatbelt as she punched the gas. On the radio, he updated the team, hoping they could adjust on the fly.

Anna drove like she'd been born behind the wheel of an F1 machine. But this wasn't a controlled track or an elite vehicle. It was a stolen muscle car with any number of modifications. One wrong move and they'd slip right off the road, into a ravine. No. Not Anna.

He wouldn't doubt her like that. Couldn't afford to let that picture into his head.

She caught up to the lead car in less than a minute. The first stall point they'd planned was coming up and she was going too fast. She'd miss it, or slide off the curve trying to make it. He clamped his lips together to avoid distracting her.

"Just breathe."

Whether she meant the advice for him or her, didn't matter. He needed the reminder.

The plan was to pin them down out here, before they reached the heart of Kite Creek. Minimizing the risk to civilians had been their entire reason for taking these guys at the hideout north of town.

His knuckles turned white as she flew through the next curve. "Anna."

"I've got this."

She'd accelerated through the turn while the driver ahead had slowed considerably. Within a split second they were riding the other car's bumper. One nervous twitch from Anna or the other man would cause an accident of epic proportions.

Theo knew the average medevac response times.

"No one dies today," she said, her voice rough as the gravel along the shoulder.

"Reading minds now?"

She didn't have time to answer. The driver ahead slammed on his brakes. Anna, smooth as silk, crossed the centerline and glided around him.

Theo breathed, filled with awe and gratitude over her superb reflexes.

"Nathan should be in position now."

Theo swiveled around and caught sight of another car behind the drug runner. "You planned to box him in?"

"It was plan B," she said, her attention split between the driver behind her and the road ahead.

"I love you." He hadn't meant to say it, definitely not right now, in this moment, but it was the absolute truth.

Her lips tipped into a half smile that faded in the next instant. "Tell Bear to get the road block in place ahead of Kite Creek."

Theo made the radio call. Relieved this would all be over soon and he could get back to what was important. Anna and the future he wanted with her.

She swore under her breath. He swiveled around, only to get thrown into the door as she jerked the wheel.

"He's trying to pass," she explained. "Can't have that."

No, that would give him a chance to hurt civilians if he busted through the road block ahead. "Can you hold him off?"

"Yes."

Her jaw was tight, but her hands were relaxed on the wheel. How did she manage that? Nathan followed the driver so closely that he couldn't pull a U-turn at this speed.

The drug runner's only hope was to get by Anna. She swerved right and left, blocking his attempts. For a short stretch of road, it seemed to be taking forever as Nathan kept the man speeding and Anna refused to let him get around.

They were close enough that Theo could see the other man screaming, but there was too much movement for him to get a clean shot at the man's tires. He resigned himself that he was only along for the ride.

"Relax," she said.

They took a direct hit from the drug runner. The seatbelt jerked him back into the seat. No airbags deployed. One of those handy modifications for speed, he was sure.

Great. If they went over now there was no hope of survival.

"Relax," Anna repeated.

Another hit shoved them forward, but Anna yanked hard on the wheel and used the extra force to her advantage, bringing her car around and up against the drug runner's vehicle.

Inch by inch, she forced him closer to the mountain, away from the dangerous drop off.

Theo saw the flashing lights of the road block and realized with a surge of relief that she'd done it. The spike strips had been deployed. Emergency crews were at the ready. This chase would come to a safe end and they'd have someone to interrogate.

The vehicles jerked and skidded to a stop just yards away from the Welcome to Kite Creek sign at the north edge of town as the tires on both vehicles were shredded by the spike strip.

"You did it."

She grinned. "We did it. Go on." She gave him a light push as the driver in the other car tried to run.

Theo launched himself from the car and tackled the man. Minutes later the guy was in handcuffs, arguing as Theo read him his rights before they tucked him into the back of a South Dakota state police vehicle. It took a bit more time to coordinate the transfer of the drugs he'd initially seized at the accident site a few weeks ago.

Returning to the car Anna had been driving, he found the trunk being inventoried by Deputy West and representatives of two other agencies. Anna wasn't there.

He scanned the chaotic scene, his heart in his throat until he spotted her in conversation with Nathan and Bear. Theo jogged up to give them his thanks for the assist before deftly drawing Anna aside. "You've given your statement?" he asked.

"Yes." She nodded without meeting his gaze. "They know where to find me for any follow up questions."

"Find you?" The realization hit him, stealing his breath. "You're leaving," he rasped.

"I-I have to." She pressed her lips together and shoved her hands into her jacket pockets. "You're safe. My job is done. There are reports and—"

"And your life as a bodyguard in Chicago," he finished for her.

"That's right."

"That's what you want?"

She nodded.

Then why were tears brimming in her big brown eyes?

He'd said he'd loved her. Sure, his timing had been lousy but the sentiment was real. If she didn't believe him, if she could write it off that kind of confession as the stress or drama of the moment, how would he ever convince her?

"All right." He tried to smile. "You've been a huge help. Thank you." Without her, he might've been killed trying to save Kite Creek. He pulled her into a hug and just held on, breathing her in.

It couldn't be the last time he held her. He vowed to himself that it wouldn't be. There was so much between them that surpassed stress and crisis. He just had to find a way to prove it to her.

Releasing her, he ignored his responsibilities to drink in every moment as she walked away, climbed into her truck, and drove out of sight.

CHAPTER 11

Anna couldn't sleep.

Chicago should've felt like coming home. It *was* home. But for two days now she'd tossed and turned in her bed. More than once she caught herself reaching for Theo in the night. The traffic sounds outside her building felt intrusive and the occasional sirens might as well be nails on a chalkboard.

She couldn't go on like this.

When her alarm went off, she silenced it, relieved that she could finally get up and go to the office. With luck, her request wouldn't be dismissed out of hand. It wasn't like they didn't have protectors stationed all over the country for quick responses. And if Gamble and Swann told her no, she could manage as Shane's mechanic. As long as Theo was in her life, she could manage anything.

"Come in." Gamble smiled as he waved her forward.

Anna stepped just inside the office doorway, too nervous to sit. "Hi. I was wondering if you've connected Coffey to the drug runners up in Kite Creek."

"We're running it down." Gamble's brow dipped into a hard scowl. "No one believes that relay crew just happened to land on his property by chance."

"Of course not." But that kind of research wasn't part of her skillset. She couldn't help with those details. Clearing her throat, she braced for the real reason she was here. "I'd like to put in for a change of address." Her knees were weak, but her voice was steady.

"Let me guess." He leaned back in his chair. "Kite Creek?"

She nodded.

Gamble's expression eased as he studied her. "You're sure?"

"It would be the best of both worlds," she said in a rush as her heart hammered. "Assuming Theo will have me," she admitted. "I'm close enough to come back if you need me in the city—"

"Leave the personnel issues to me," Gamble interjected. He tapped a pen on a folder. "We can work out something," he said. "You're one of the best we have on the roster and I'm not willing to give you up completely if we can compromise."

Hope weakened her knees and she sank into the chair. "Thank you."

"Can I get your opinion on a potential new hire while you're here? He's applying as a driver."

"Sure." She'd happily cooperate. She owed Gamble and Swann for giving her a chance to find her footing in a career she'd come to love. She gasped at the name and photo on the application. "Theo applied for a job here?"

"He did. Spoke with me this morning about it. He's interviewing with Swann and the boss right now."

"But…but he loves Kite Creek. He's an excellent sheriff." Devoted, honest. A hot flash of anger prickled under her skin. "They need him up there."

"And you?"

Well. "I need him too," she confessed in a whisper. "Not in Chicago. He hates the city." She didn't like it much herself after being with him in the Black Hills. "He's the reason I want to move to Kite Creek."

Gamble's gaze narrowed. "Does he know that?"

"He should." But how could he? She hadn't responded when he'd said he loved her. She hadn't even kissed him goodbye. Hadn't dared. She was a coward, especially when it came to relationships. "I need to tell him."

"He's still the sheriff of record. Hasn't given his notice yet."

"He hasn't?"

"No." Gamble watched her, his lips twitching as if a smile would break loose any second. "Anna, go get your man. He's in the small conference room."

"Thanks." She dashed out of the office. There was still a chance it would all fall apart, but if he was willing to return to a major city, for her, surely there was reason to hope.

Anna braced for rejection as she pulled open the door of the conference room. She and Theo had been through so much in such a short amount of time. It had to mean something that he was here and she wanted to be there.

"Anna?" Swann's expression was eerily close to his partner's. A little smug and edging toward happiness.

"Pardon the interruption." She looked to the device on the center of the table, concerned that the firm's most eccentric client was on the line for the interview.

"It's just the two of us," Swann said. "What do you need?"

"Theo lied on his application," she blurted.

"Anna." Theo said her name like a sigh.

She didn't dare look at him until they were alone. "He isn't qualified to drive for the Guardian Agency. He drives like an old lady."

"Anna!" Theo surged to his feet and came to a stop right in front of her. "I'm trying to do what's best for you."

She looked up into his handsome face, fighting back a rush of tears. "But I want to do what's best for *us*."

"I'll give you two a minute," Swann said, ducking out of the room.

"You hate the city," Anna accused when they were alone.

"You love it," he countered. "I'll adapt."

"I don't love it anymore." Her hands toyed with the buttons of his shirt, right over his heart. "I can't sleep."

"Why not?"

"The noise is ridiculous. And there were no songbirds this morning."

He stepped back, folding his arms over his chest. "Noise. Is that all?"

She cracked her knuckles. "No, not all." She met his gaze, had to be brave. "You weren't beside me. I need you, Theo." She swallowed. "I love you and I need you."

He didn't budge, so she stepped closer and pulled his arms around her waist. "I love you," she repeated. "Say it back. Please."

His eyes danced and a slow smile spread over his face. He kissed her lightly on the lips. "I'm here. For you. Because I love you."

Happy tears rolled down her cheeks. He'd said it before and she'd been sure it had just been the intensity of the situation. This time, she knew exactly how much he meant it.

"Your turn," he urged.

"I love you." She pressed up on her toes and kissed him, slowly. "And you belong in Kite Creek," she murmured against his lips. She skimmed her hands down his arms to lace her fingers through his. "And I belong wherever you are. If you'll have me."

"Shouldn't that be my question?" He kissed her forehead. "No Chinese food or pizza delivery in Kite Creek," he reminded her.

"I know a guy who makes homemade pizza to die for."

"That good?"

"Truly." She gave his hands a squeeze. "Don't do this. Don't leave everything you've built for me."

"But you're everything, Anna. My heart, my future. All right here with you."

"Theo." Her heart was a puddle of happiness in her chest. "I was giving Gamble my change of address. As a protector I can live anywhere and commute as needed for the job."

"Really?"

She grinned at the glint of hope in his gaze. "I had it all worked out in my head. It would've been a grand gesture as I swept back into town and proposed to you at Patty's."

His eyebrows arched. "You were planning to propose?"

"Yes. Please marry me, Theo. I never thought I'd find someone who understood me, who made me better at being me. I love you and I trust you to love me back. Forever."

His sexy smile sent a delicious thrill through her system. "Is that a yes?" she pressed.

"Pushy," he teased. "Do you have a ring?"

Only the one she always wore. "For you?" She bit her lip. "No. Not on me."

"Good thing I do." He pulled a small velvet covered box from his pocket. A gorgeous round diamond, clear and deep, glittered up at her.

"You bought me a ring." It was too beautiful to touch, almost too good to be real.

"This is yes, Anna." He took the ring from the box and slipped it onto her finger. "Yes, I'll marry you. The rest of my days are yours, my love."

She gawked at the gorgeous solitaire diamond in a setting that complimented the heirloom she'd worn most of her life. Theo slid the engagement ring over her finger. It was a perfect fit, as if she'd been made to wear it.

"Anna?" He tipped up her chin until she met his gaze. "Second thoughts?"

"Never. Let's go home."

"Mine or yours?"

"Can your place be ours?" She held out her hand, admiring the play of light on the diamond. "Patty and Grandpa Cahill will come after me if I don't get you back to the sheriff's station by morning. That's not a good first impression."

"We can't have that." He kissed her again, and once more for good measure before they walked out of the conference room.

To their mutual surprise, the hallway was packed with Gamble, Swann and the staff that supported the law firm and the Guardian Agency. Everyone broke into cheers as Anna flashed the ring and announced their engagement.

She linked her hand with his, savoring the best first moment of the rest of her life with the man of her dreams at her side.

The End

Lost Signal

Off The Radar

For full details on all of Regan's books visit ReganBlack.com and

enjoy excerpts from each of her sexy, adrenaline-fueled novels.

Deadly Observations

Deadly Reflections, Behind Closed Doors series

Black Ice, Stormwatch series

what she knew, Book 4 in Breakdown, a multi-author series

Knight Traveler Series

The Matchmaker Series

Escape Club Heroes, Harlequin Romantic Suspense

The Riley Code, Harlequin Romantic Suspense

Colton Family saga, a multi-author series, Harlequin Romantic Suspense

ABOUT REGAN BLACK

Regan Black, a USA Today and internationally bestselling author, writes award-winning, action-packed romances featuring kick-butt heroines and the sexy heroes who fall in love with them. Raised in the Midwest and California, she and her husband share their empty nest with two adorably arrogant cats in the South Carolina Lowcountry where the rich blend of legend, romance, and history fuels her imagination.

For free reads, exclusive prizes, and much more, subscribe to the monthly newsletter at Regan-Black.com/perks.

Keep up with Regan online:
www.ReganBlack.com
Facebook
Instagram

Or follow Regan at:
BookBub
Amazon

facebook.com/ReganBlack.fans
instagram.com/reganblackauthor

ELLE JAMES also writing as MYLA JACKSON is a *New York Times* and *USA Today* Bestselling author of books including cowboys, intrigues and paranormal adventures that keep her readers on the edges of their seats. With over one hundred and eighty works in a variety of sub-genres and lengths she has published with Harlequin, Samhain, Ellora's Cave, Kensington, Cleis Press, and Avon. When she's not at her computer, she's traveling, reading or riding her ATV, dreaming up new stories. Learn more about Elle James at www.ellejames.com

Website | Facebook | Twitter | GoodReads | Newsletter | BookBub | Amazon

Follow Elle!
www.ellejames.com
ellejames@ellejames.com

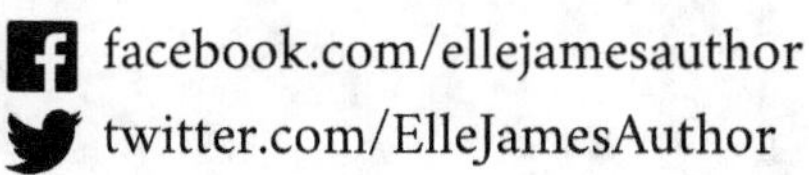
facebook.com/ellejamesauthor
twitter.com/ElleJamesAuthor

www.ingramcontent.com/pod-product-compliance
Lightning Source LLC
Chambersburg PA
CBHW071949150726